raising kane

Dana Goldstein

ISBN (paperback) 978-1-0699388-0-0

ISBN (ebook) 978-1-0699388-1-7

*For the family I chose
and the family I built.*

ruth

"RUTH? CAN YOU HEAR ME?"

I was sitting up, strapped to a gurney, when the back of the ambulance opened. Hands reached in, and I was bounced and jostled out. As we crashed through the doors marked Emergency, voices came at me from every direction. Words I didn't comprehend but knew they were about me.

"Why are we here?" I mumbled. I tilted my head back to look at the paramedic pushing the gurney from behind.

She flicked her eyes down to me, then diverted her attention to a nurse who appeared out of nowhere, clipboard in hand, taking notes.

"Vitals?" the nurse asked.

"Blood pressure and pulse stable. Pulse ox a bit low. No obvious signs of trauma. Likely in shock." The words rolled off the paramedic's tongue as easily as prayers rolled off mine. I closed my eyes, trying not to move my lips as I prayed that the others were spared. I went to that place in my head, the one filled with light and hope that always took me somewhere else for a while.

I replayed the last time Mom and Dad and I were all together. We were planting the winter wheat, each of us in our row, working through the repetitive motion of dig, drop, bury as we seeded our assigned portion of the field. Mom started singing her favorite song, "Ain't No Mountain High Enough," and Dad and I joined in at the chorus. Her voice was soothing, helping me forget about the dirt under my nails and the ache in my back. Dad sang off-key on purpose just to make me laugh.

I became aware of a muffled voice calling my name again, separating me from the memory. I raised my hands to my ears, sure I would find cotton balls stuffed in them.

"Ruth? Can you hear me? Ruth?"

I was freezing. I wasn't wearing my dress anymore. Instead,

my body was covered in stiff fabric. The smell of urine over-whelmed me. My chest squeezed with fear. Where was I?

A sharp sting in my left arm brought me back to myself. All at once, everything consumed me. The pain. The smells. The cold. The screaming.

From behind the masked face hovering over me, the words became clear.

"Can you hear me?"

I nodded. I turned my head, taking in the beige walls, the swarm of gowned bodies, and the machines.

"Do you know where you are?"

My mouth was so dry my tongue was a thick, dead piece of flesh. Even my teeth hurt, something I didn't know was possible. Before I could work out how to connect my brain to my words, the mask turned away.

I wanted to answer, but something cool flooded into my arm, and I felt myself slipping away. Again.

I wanted to tell someone in this room that I knew. I wanted them to know that before we moved to a village in Idaho, before I was quiet and obedient and called Ruth, I was someone else. As a calm, comforting sleep wrapped around me, I reached down to scratch an itchy spot on my leg. My fingers grazed a scar near my ankle, the one I got from the rough bark of a tree I climbed a long time ago. I rubbed the scar and remembered. I was Zoe then.

one

MOM and I were outside the trailer, both of us kneeling in the prayer zone facing the falling sun. Mom chose this spot, the calm and quiet of sunset allowing us to focus on our gratitude prayers. The gravel covering the square area dug into my knees, but I didn't really feel it anymore. After seven years of praying outside every evening, I wasn't bothered so much by the little stones or the coming darkness.

Before we finished the third of our four evening prayers, we heard popping, like firecrackers. *Pop, pop, pop, pop, pop, pop.* Six times, I subconsciously counted. Then the sounds of *crack, boom, crack, boom, crack* filled the air. Five times, I counted in my head. I knew it was a shotgun.

Mom leapt up from the prayer pad and ran around the front of the trailer, tiny pebbles shaking themselves loose from her knees and leaving a trail. More popping and booming and cracking. And then the yelling started. Not just yelling but screaming and crying too. And begging. I thought I heard Hannah pleading, "Please, please, please," before I didn't hear my best friend anymore. The air went from smelling of fresh pine to sickly sweet and smoky. I knew the smell of fire, but there was something I couldn't quite identify mixed in with the smoke.

Mom ran back to me, pulling me up by the fleshy part under my right arm.

"Ow," I protested, "that hurts."

My mother's eyes were everywhere but on me.

"You need to go," Mom hissed.

"Go where?"

"Anywhere but here." Mom had scurried back to the front of the trailer, peering around the rounded end.

"Mom, what's going on?" I asked. No response. "Mom? MOM?" I screeched.

My mother only turned her head to gaze at me, looking like she didn't know who was speaking.

"Mom?" I whispered. "What's happening?"

My mother shook her head before hissing a single word.

"Run."

Mom grabbed me by the shoulders, turning me away from the trailer before giving me a rough push. I stumbled from the unexpected shove but managed to keep my feet on the ground. When I turned back to the trailer, Mom was gone.

The air squeezed out of my lungs, and tears sprang to my eyes. I was alone and afraid and didn't know what to do. I stood rooted to the spot, my heart pounding in my chest, as gray smoke drifted around me, blocking out the trailer's porch light. Voices drifted over what sounded like glass shattering, people calling for help or wailing at someone to stop.

Even though my gut told me I shouldn't, I walked around the front of the trailer, hoping to find my mother on the other side. When I saw the wall of flames engulfing some of the other trailers and the smoke changing from white to thick black plumes, I did exactly what Mom had told me to do.

I ran.

I fled to the only place I could think of to hide: under the raised chicken coop at the southern edge of the wheat field. In my panic, I tripped on the hens' entry ramp and felt something pop in my left ankle. I crawled under, scraping my forearm on loose chicken wire. Blood bloomed instantly, and I smeared it away with my dirty palm. Shivering against the November chill, I rolled onto my side, curling my legs into my stomach.

The sun had sunk behind the mountains, shrouding everything in darkness. My other senses came alive. I held my breath, listening for voices. All I heard now was the crackle and hiss of fire. Curtains of smoke billowed around me, and I buried my chin into the crook of my elbow, trying to stifle my coughing. I lay there, waiting for my parents to come find me. I had to pee, but there was no way I was coming out from under the coop. To distract myself, I searched for patterns in the stained wood above me. There, near my right shoulder, was a puppy's face. At my hip, I saw the shape of a seal, sitting up with its front flippers in the air.

I lay there, listening to the crackling get softer until there was no sound at all. No more pops or booms. Not a hoot of an owl. Not a single voice. I whispered a prayer for the others. When I closed my eyes, I saw my mother's face, filled with fear and something else I didn't recognize.

I squeezed my eyes tight and tried to make a telepathic connection with my mother.

Mom? Why aren't you looking for me? You told me to run. I listened, and now you're not here. Did you forget about me? Please come get me. I promise I'll be good. I want to finish our prayers.

I listened carefully, straining to hear anything. Wind blew over and under the coop, carrying that sickening smoke to my nose. I had no idea what was happening in the village, but in the silence, I sensed something awful.

two

I MUST HAVE DRIFTED off because my eyes flew open as soon as I heard unfamiliar voices. I drew my legs tighter into my chest to make myself as small as possible. I tested my breathing to make sure I wouldn't be heard. If I breathed through my nose, there was the tiniest whistling; if I breathed through my mouth, I could control the sound.

As the voices got louder, I was able to pinpoint where they were coming from: the north side of the wheat field, which meant the owners of the voices had passed through the village.

"I've never seen anything like it," I heard a male voice say.

"Me neither," said a woman. "Not in my ten years on the squad."

"You read about these things on the internet and you see it on TV, but man …"

"Someone swept through here like a tornado on a rampage."

I took a quick and quiet deep breath and held it. I squeezed my eyes tight to eliminate the temptation to peek out from under the coop. I could hear them approaching, the crunch of frozen earth giving way to the scrape of gravel. I felt the air change near my head as the bodies attached to the voices neared. The wire door of the coop squeaked open.

"This has been empty for a while," the woman said. "I can still smell the crap, though."

Don't move, don't move, don't move. Wait for Mom to find you.

The voices again drifted from the back of the coop. I opened my eyes, watching two sets of black and yellow boots, shiny like plastic, but with a rougher texture. With every step, gravel and dust kicked up around me.

Don't sneeze. Don't sneeze. Don't sneeze.

I held my breath again as they passed and managed not to breathe in any dust. But it was my stomach that betrayed me, groaning with hunger.

One set of boots stopped moving.

"Did you hear that?" The woman.

The other boots stopped. I wrapped my arms around my belly, hoping to muffle the sound if it happened again. When it did, I brought my legs even closer to my chest and shut my eyes, trying to shrink myself to nothing.

"Hey there," the woman said, her voice now much closer to me. "It's OK. I'm not going to hurt you."

Dark brown eyes were looking at me when I opened my own. The woman was on her knees, peering at me under the coop. She took off her firefighter's helmet and pushed what looked like a faceless ski mask off her head. Her short, copper-red hair was plastered to her head.

"Are you hurt?" she asked.

As soon as she asked that, pain flared up from my ankle. My whole foot felt like it was on fire. I lifted my head a bit off the ground and nodded.

"OK," she said. She swept her eyes over me, taking in the scratch on my arm and the scrapes on my legs from the gravel. "Do you feel safe enough to come out of there?"

I blinked. I was scared and cold. These outsiders had been through the village. Did they know where my parents were? Where was everyone else? The smoke had cleared, but right then I knew. Something really bad had happened.

The woman's eyes met mine for a second and then she stood

up. I couldn't see what she was doing, but a second later, a heavy yellow jacket covered in soot hit the ground. When the firefighter kneeled again, she wasn't wearing her coat anymore.

"You must be cold," she said, pushing the jacket toward me. "This will be big enough to cover you past your knees, I think. I'm Courtney, by the way." She smiled, giving the jacket another gentle push.

I reached out to pull the jacket over me. It was heavy and smelled like campfire, but it didn't really warm me up. I could feel air moving across my torso. I lost control of my body and started shivering. My full bladder emptied. I was almost sixteen years old, and I had just peed myself.

Courtney stood up again, and I heard her say, "We need a paramedic over here!"

The man said, "On it," and moved away from the coop.

"I have a daughter about your age," she said, coming back down to my level. She wasn't just kneeling now; she was actually lying on the ground beside me.

I pulled the jacket up higher so the stiff collar sat right below my chin. I could feel her eyes on me but avoided looking at her. I was cold and confused. I wanted my mom.

"Do you feel ready to come out?" she asked.

Ignoring the searing pain in my ankle, I flipped over onto my hands and knees and crawled out from under the coop. I sat on the cold ground, my knees to my chest again, and pulled the jacket around me. I didn't trust my legs to be able to hold me after lying down for so long.

Courtney nodded. "OK, this is good. Can you stand up?"

I shrugged.

"Want to try? You can grab onto me. I'll hold you up."

She stood and held out her hand. I lifted my own and noticed it was cut and filthy and spotted with blood. I pulled my hand back, embarrassed by my dirty state.

"It's fine." Courtney smiled down at me. "A little dirt and blood doesn't bother me. I work with a bunch of boys. You know how gross they are?"

I wanted to smile back, but I couldn't make my mouth move that way. I immediately thought of my brother and how he used to stink after playing hockey, and my heart filled with so much sadness. Everything changed after he died, but I was glad he was not part of whatever happened out there in the village. The fire would not touch him.

I put my hands on either side of my legs and started to push up. Courtney reached down and gently pulled me under my elbow. I hissed as pain shot through my ankle again. I grasped at Courtney.

"You OK?" she asked. I shook my head.

"My ankle ..." I croaked. My throat was raspy, raw from the smoke.

I let myself be lifted, putting all my weight on my right leg. I wobbled, trying to find my balance.

We heard an engine coming from behind the barn and we waited, our breath pluming from our mouths. Just above the barn roof, the glow from the fire had been replaced with the radiance of sunrise. I had been out all night.

An ambulance came around the side of the barn, stopping next to the chicken coop. A paramedic climbed out of the front passenger seat.

"Come on to the back," he said. "We've got warm blankets."

I let Courtney lead the way. The doors at the rear of the ambulance were already open, and a second paramedic, also a woman, stood there, holding something silver. I let myself be wrapped in the thermal blanket, then leaned back onto a gurney. The smell of urine wafted off my body, and I squeezed my legs together, hoping to contain the foul odor. It didn't seem to bother the paramedic as she looked me over, listening to my heart and my lungs, and then she let me listen too. I could hear the steady *tharump tharump* of my heart and the *whoof whoof* of my lungs.

"Can you tell us your name?" Courtney asked.

I watched the curly black hair on the top of the paramedic's head as she kneeled beside me, gently examining my bruised and swollen ankle.

"Ru …" I sputtered. Even after seven years, the name still felt weird, like I had a giant gumball in my mouth.

"Ru?" Courtney repeated.

I shook my head. Swallowed. Forced the name off my tongue.

"Ruth," I croaked, surprised by the grittiness of my voice. "What … where are my parents?"

When Courtney glanced at the paramedic, I knew. It had been long enough for my parents to come looking for me, but there was no one.

"I'm going to leave you in Shaylene's capable hands, Ruth," Courtney murmured, ignoring my question. She squeezed my hand before closing the back doors. Shaylene took a seat on the bench across from me, letting the other paramedic take the wheel.

As we drove toward the main gate of the village, I saw my world retreating through the back windows of the ambulance. The wheat field was blackened. All that remained were the smoking shells of trailers. Everything smoldered, burned beyond recognition.

Once we pulled onto the main road leading away from the village, bright lights began to flash. People swarmed around the ambulance, and I instinctively ducked, turning away from the windows to hide from the noise and chaos. Camera shutters clicked and voices shouted questions. Suddenly, the sirens blared to life in short bursts. Shaylene leapt to her feet, standing in front of me, protectively blocking my face from prying eyes.

As the ambulance continued moving, the noise around me died down. I lifted my head and saw we were heading to a field that had been roped off with bright yellow ribbon. When we passed, I caught sight of the words *Police Line*. Parked on the brown grass were two black-and-white police cars, three firetrucks, three ambulances, and a white bus.

"What is that?" I asked.

"That is an ambulance bus," she told me, sitting back on the bench. "It's for situations where there are multiple injuries."

"But there is no one in there." As soon as the words left my mouth, the meaning of the empty bus became clear. I looked down at my fingernails, each clogged with dirt. *This can't be happening. I must be dreaming.*

Shaylene sighed. "That's right, Ruth."

"Are they coming? Who is helping my friends?"

Shaylene breathed in through her nose.

"We haven't found anyone else yet. Why were you hiding under the chicken coop? To get away from the fire?"

"My mom told me to run away." My eyes filled with tears, and I let them fall. There was no reason for me to be brave. "Are my parents dead?"

"Sweetie," she started, leaning forward and pushing my hair behind my ear, "we don't know exactly what happened to your parents. Do you?"

I shook my head. "It's bad, isn't it? Is every … everyone … de—dead?"

"I don't know. Let's just take care of you right now."

"Am I the only one alive?"

three

I MUST HAVE BLACKED OUT, because the next time I opened my eyes, I was alone and lying flat on my back. That's how I knew I wasn't in my own bed. I'm a side sleeper, and I couldn't feel the down of my mattress hugging my hip. Whatever I was lying on had no real cushioning. When I sat up, my head swirled with dizziness, turning all my senses into a fuzzy haze.

The light around and above me was a filtered gray. Above the bed, a soft glow leaked around the edges of a blind covering a window. It was daytime. Still or again, I couldn't be sure. Sound came to my ears slowly, beeping and the murmur of voices somewhere nearby.

In a rush of recall, I remembered I was in the hospital. I replayed my last hours at the village, before I was found hiding under the empty coop, stinking of smoke and my own urine.

I lay back on the hospital bed, the pillow crinkling under my head, like it was made of plastic. I wanted my brain to stay in the fog for a bit longer. I examined the ceiling tiles, noticing a dark stain left by a water leak. My lids were heavy, calling me back to sleep.

The curtain in front of the glass door at the end of the bed whooshed open, and two women walked in. The one in front was short, about the same height as me, wearing a white lab coat, with a stethoscope draped around her neck. On her head, she wore a light blue cap, elasticized at the edges, hugging her skull and hiding most of her hair.

"Ruth. I'm Dr. DiPaolo, and this is Nurse Carolina. We're here to examine you. Would that be OK?"

"Yes," I rasped. My tongue was working again, but my throat felt like I had swallowed glass.

"When was the last time you saw a doctor?" Dr. DiPaolo asked as she wrapped a cuff around my upper left arm.

"I'm not sure." I shrugged. We only went to see Dr. Zion when our own home remedies failed. "Ow." I flinched as the cuff squeezed my arm. I watched my flesh compress and noticed the thumbprint bruise where my mother had pinched me. My eyes burned, tears threatening to fall again. My blood pounded in my head.

"It only squeezes for a second," Carolina said, taking my right hand in hers and rubbing the top.

I sat silently as they poked and prodded at me, doing the same things the paramedic did in the ambulance. They took my blood, made me pee in a cup, and examined every part of my body. It was uncomfortable and embarrassing and unpleasant.

"All done," Dr. DiPaolo said, peeling the gloves off her hands with a snapping noise. "Your ankle is badly bruised, but it's not broken or sprained. Do you have any questions?"

"Are my parents here? Can I see my mom?"

The doctor and the nurse exchanged a quick glance, and that's when I knew for sure. No one was coming to get me.

"May I sit?" Dr. DiPaolo asked, pointing to the bed.

I moved my legs to the side to make room. The doctor sat at the foot of the bed. The nurse closed the glass door and pulled the curtain in front.

"Ruth, I'm so very sorry to have to tell you this, but no one else survived the fire."

Instantly, I was lightheaded and dizzy. I wanted the blackness to take me again.

"No one?" I whispered. I shook my head, trying to deny the confirmation of speaking this out loud.

Maybe Abigail and James and Noah and Hannah ran to the woods. Maybe my friends are just fine. They'll be here any minute.

"I'm really sorry." Dr. DiPaolo put her hand on my leg. I flinched, and she pulled her hand away. "Family services will be sending someone as soon as they can."

The panic inside me must have washed over my face.

"Medically, you'll be just fine, Ruth. It might not feel that way, but with the right help, you'll work through this. Our bodies and our brains are remarkable machines," she said. "Someone will be right back to help you get cleaned up." She patted my leg and walked out of the room. Carolina gave me a thin-lipped smile before she followed. I was alone again.

A blanket was folded at the end of the bed. When I sat up to reach for it, I recoiled from the smell still coming off my body. I was covered in dirt and grime and urine. I lay down, rolling onto my side, and pulled the blanket over my head. The smell was awful, but familiar.

Cocooned in my own stench, I bargained with a god I had prayed to for the past seven years but had never seen. *I'll do anything to have things back the way they were. I won't think about being Zoe ever again. I don't want to go back to Montana. I swear. Please let my parents be alive. I want to go home.*

Home. That didn't exist for me anymore. I saw what I saw from the back of that ambulance. There wasn't a single trailer or building left for me to go back to. There was no one left to catch me, to raise me up like they did when we first moved to the village and our names were changed.

In the light filtering through the thin blanket, I turned my arm to examine the mark my mother left me. I put my own thumb over the bruise, rubbing it, relishing the tenderness and pain. I never wanted this last connection to my mom to fade.

The nurse who came in next didn't say much, but she gave me a look I'd seen a ton after my brother died. It was a look that said *I'm sad for you, but I know I can't do anything to make you hurt less, and I don't know what to say.* Her arms were crossed over her ID badge, making it impossible for me to read her name. I did catch sight of a few words, though: Eastern Idaho Regional.

"Follow me," was all she said. Spinning in her clogs, she left the room.

I followed her down the hall, avoiding eye contact with anyone else. I knew I smelled horrible. It felt like I'd been parading for miles before she stopped at a room with a light-colored wood door.

"You can shower in here. I'll be over there at that desk." She pointed down the hall to her right. "Come find me when you're finished."

I opened the door and turned back to tell her I had nothing to change into, but she was already gone. I moved into the wide space, seeing a pile of folded towels and washcloths, as well as a clean, white robe hanging from a hook. The soap and shampoo came from dispensers attached to the wall. I turned on the shower, adjusted it to as hot as I could tolerate, and stood under the water. It felt so good, the little needles of spray comforting on my back.

I stood there for a long time before I started washing. I shampooed my hair twice, then let it sit in a soapy pile on top of my head. Both the shampoo and the soap smelled like pine needles and cough medicine mixed together. I lathered up a washcloth and began with my face, moving down to my neck and arms. When I looked at the washcloth, it was black with dirt. I tossed it into a bin with other dirty towels and took another washcloth. It took fifteen washcloths to get myself clean, one for every year of my life. I emerged from the shower, feeling like a human being again, scrubbed clean on the outside.

I looked at myself in the mirror, and my breath caught in my throat. I hadn't looked in a proper mirror for the last seven years. *Vanity is for those with weak minds*, Abraham always said. With the towel wrapped around my head, wisps of my dark brown hair showing at my temples, the shape of my face was more obvious. The last time I gazed at my reflection, my cheeks were still plump with baby fat. The girl in this mirror had a longer face, with gently sloping cheekbones and a soft, rounded chin. I looked into my own eyes, still dark brown with flecks of gold, and saw someone unfamiliar.

A ripple of the unknown ran through me. I could walk out of this shower room with a clean slate. With no family and an empty history, I could be whoever I wanted to be. It wasn't just the dirt gone from my skin. I could scrub Ruth away too.

four

I FOUND the nurse at the desk as promised. I could see her ID badge and her name. Lin. She smiled up at me, then closed the magazine she'd been reading. On the cover was a couple dressed in formal wear, their smiles revealing perfectly straight and unnaturally white teeth. *Star Gazing*, the title read. The confusion must have been clear on my face, because the nurse laughed and flipped it over.

"There's not much time to dig into a book here." She smiled. "Only quick hits of entertainment, I'm afraid. Nothing requires less attention than the love lives of the rich and famous. Do you think those two will ever get married?"

I stared at her, trying hard to understand what, and who, she was talking about.

"Oh god." She blushed, acknowledging my blank stare. "You have no idea what I'm talking about. These two ... they're actors ... dating forever ... uh ... you know what? It doesn't matter."

Her eyes traveled from my head to my waist, taking in my shoulder-length hair, the bags under my eyes, and the fact that I was still wearing a bathrobe.

"OK, let's get you back to your room, and I'll find you something to eat. Sound good?"

I couldn't remember the last time I had eaten. Even though my stomach was flat and tight with emptiness, I was uninterested in food.

The bed had been made while I was gone. I sat down on the

fresh sheets, overcome by the fatigue washing through every part of my body. My legs and arms were heavy. As the nurse checked my blood pressure again, I listened to my breathing, the steady rasp in and out of my nose. But there would be no sleep for me. My brain was buzzing, flickering through what had happened over the last—I glanced at the clock on the wall—eighteen hours.

Had it really been less than a day?

There was a soft knock at the door, and a man pushed the curtain partway open, poking his head inside.

"Hi, Ruth? I'm Gary. I'm from family services. Is it OK if I come in?"

"Hey, Gary," Lin said before I could answer. "Long time, no see. I've known Gary for almost twenty years," she said, looking at me, tearing open the Velcro on the blood pressure cuff. "Do you want me to stay with you?"

I flicked my eyes over to this stranger at the door. His salt-and-pepper hair was short and sticking up from the top of his head. I took in the long-sleeve shirt buttoned at the collar, the pullover vest, the faded blue jeans. His glasses seemed to be too small for his wide, round face. His eyes were hazel, the same color as Hannah's. *As Hannah's were*, I reminded myself. A door slid closed inside me.

"It's fine," I said. Lin nodded and walked out of the room.

"I've brought you some clothes to change into, if you want," Gary said, holding up the handles of a large brown paper bag. "We weren't sure what you would feel comfortable in, so here's a variety of things." He named each item as he placed it on the high-back chair in the corner. Shirts. Jeans. Sweatpants. Dress. Socks. Underwear.

"What size shoe do you wear?"

I hadn't even noticed I'd lost my shoes somewhere along the way.

"Size seven, I think." This was the size that fit the last time I'd gotten shoes from our community closet.

"OK, I'll go rustle up some sevens."

When he left the room, I pushed off the bed and shuffled to the chair to examine the clothes. I picked up the sweatpants first. They were so soft, I was tempted to rub them against my face. The T-shirts were just as soft. The jeans had a label, were faded and stretchy, yet invited me to pull them on. I wanted to wear everything. Where did these clothes come from? Why was there so much? Abraham's voice drifted back into my head. *People out there only collect things with the intent of disposing of them. They pursue temporary happiness.*

I shook his words away and threw a baggy sweatshirt over my head. The softness of the sweatpants called to me, but I really wanted to slip my legs into the jeans. When I pulled the denim over my scrawny hips, another memory slammed into me.

"They always feel rough when they come out of the wash," my mother told a six-year-old me. "But after you wear them for a bit, they get soft and loose again."

I sank into the chair, feeling the hole in my heart. I was never going to hear her voice again. How long would it be before her last word—*Run!*—faded from my mind? I leaned over, face in my hands, and let the tears spill into my palms.

five

I **WAS** a disgusting mess of snot and tears when Gary returned to my room. He slid the door closed and pulled the curtain, shutting out the noise in the ward.

"Are you up to talking yet? I can come back later if you need more time."

I shook my head, then nodded. I needed to know what was going to happen to me.

"I see you found some clothes that fit. That's good," he said, leaning his shoulder against the wall beside the bed. "I found these in the gift shop."

I wiped my eyes and nose with my palms. Gary handed me a pair of dark blue slip-ons made of soft, squishy plastic. They felt like clouds looked. "Thanks. How long will I be in the hospital?"

"Not long. Dr. DiPaolo says you check out OK, but she wants to keep you for one more night."

"And then what? Where will I go?" I could feel the panic building from my stomach to my chest, like phantom hands twisting my insides.

"That's what we need to talk about, Ruth. Do you have any other family?"

I started to shake my head but stopped. I hadn't seen my grandmother since we left Montana, after my brother died from cancer. Was she even still alive?

"I had a grandmother when we lived in Billings."

"Do you remember her name?"

I nodded. "Lottie."

"Is Lottie short for Loretta?"

"I don't know. She was always just Grandma Lottie."

"OK, we can start the search with that."

Were they going to track her down and make me live with her? Of course they would. But what if she couldn't be found? Dad never talked about her, not once in seven years. I figured that meant she was dead too.

My eyes burned with fresh tears, but now there was a flare of anger. How could my parents abandon me like this? Did my mother know the plan? How could she think I'd be better off alive and alone?

"Ruth, there will be a lot of people who want to talk to you today," Gary said, interrupting my building anger. "Police, FBI, that sort of thing."

"Do I have to?" I snapped. *Uniforms don't demand respect,* Abraham once said, *and it's always lies passing their lips. They are not our friends, and they don't really want to help.*

"Ruth, I know you are in a world of confusion right now. But yes, you will have to speak to the authorities."

"Does it have to be today? Can't it wait?"

Gary looked directly into my eyes, but I looked away, trying to hide my fear.

"It's easier to rip off the Band-Aid right away. Talking about the hard things is part of the healing. And someone will be with you the whole time."

Gary had barely finished speaking when someone rapped on the glass door. Without waiting for a response, the door slid open and the curtain was pushed aside.

A man wearing black jeans and a button-down shirt open at the neck walked in, followed by a woman dressed in khaki pants and a navy polo. Both were wearing black parkas, the letters "FBI" embroidered on the upper left front.

"Is that her?" the man asked, motioning toward me with his chin.

"Her name is Ruth," Gary said, walking to the end of my bed, placing himself between me and these new visitors.

"Hi, Ruth. I'm sure you're really scared right now, but we're here to help," he said, without a hint of a smile. With so many people in the tiny room, claustrophobia and distrust closed around me, shielding me from the lie.

"Can you tell us what happened? What did you see? Were you aware that any of this might happen?" He barked the questions at me, making it sound like I was in trouble. My head buzzed, and I had no idea which question he wanted me to answer first.

I leaned back into the chair. Sweat gathered in the small of my back. Every instinct in my body was on alert, telling me to approach with caution. I decided it might be better if I just kept my mouth shut for now.

"Can she hear?" he asked Gary. "Why isn't she answering me?"

"Because you fired too many questions at her," Gary answered and shifted to the right, blocking me from their sight. "Give her some space. She's in shock."

"And you are?" the second agent asked.

"From family services."

"Right. So, you know the procedure."

"And you know the longer we wait, the harder our job will be," the first agent said.

"Introducing yourselves might help things along," Gary chastised. "She's not a suspect here."

The first agent held Gary's gaze for a moment before stepping around him. "Ruth, I'm Agent Daniel Miller and that"—he pointed to his partner who stood in the doorway, arms tucked behind her—"is Agent Shivani Chopra. You can call me Dan."

"And you can call me Shivani," the woman said, pressing her lips into a thin line.

They are not your friends. Keep your distance.

"Do you understand what has happened? Do you know why we are here?" Agent Dan started.

Before I answered, I reached over to the bedside table, pulling a box of tissues into my lap. I wiped my face, then blew my nose. Buying time.

"Yes," I answered.

"Can you tell us what you remember from before the firefighters found you?"

"I was cold."

"I meant before that. Where were you before you went under the coop?"

"At our trailer."

"Were you alone?"

"No."

Agent Dan glanced over at his partner before asking the next question. "Who was with you?" He pinched the bridge of his nose and closed his eyes, waiting for my answer.

"My mom."

"Ruth," Gary said, his voice gentle, "can you tell us what you and your mom were doing and why you were hiding?"

I lifted my eyes and met his. There was kindness there, and for a moment, I let a little light crack through the wall inside me.

"We were praying. And then things started happening. We heard noises that sounded like firecrackers popping—I could smell the fire before I saw it. She told me to run ..." My words stuck in my throat. I should have stayed with her. If I hadn't done as I was told, I wouldn't be all alone.

"Do you know how the fire started?"

I shook my head.

"Can you tell us who started the fire?"

Again, I shook my head.

Agent Dan sighed. "Maybe you can try," he said to his partner.

Agent Shivani walked toward the bed. She held out a photo, pointing it in my direction. "Do you know this man?"

I glanced at the photo and knew immediately this was a younger version of Abraham, our leader and the village founder.

"Abraham doesn't look like that anymore," I told her. "His hair is all silver, and he doesn't have the moustache."

The first time I met Abraham, his straight hair was black and fell to his shoulders. Over time, as the silver filled in, he started cutting it shorter. Three days ago, my parents were joking with Abraham about how his scalp was taking up more space lately.

"Any idea where he might be?"

"No."

Without invitation, Agent Shivani sat down at the end of the bed, folding her arms across her chest. I shifted back in the chair to put even more space between us.

"You're not in any trouble, Ruth. We're just trying to figure out what happened."

"So am I," I whispered. Again, tears welled up in my eyes.

There was a knock on the doorframe, and a head poked into the room.

"I have your dinner, Ruth," the man said, walking in with a tray. He glanced at the FBI agents before placing my dinner on a wheeled table pushed against the wall. The smell of scrambled eggs assaulted my nose, and I swallowed against a wave of nausea.

"I'll be back later to pick it up when you're done," he said before leaving.

"OK," Gary said, rising from the chair. "I think that's enough for now."

Agent Shivani glanced at her partner, who was looking at Gary with an irritated expression.

"Fine," he relented, "but I need to take some photos for distribution. Would that be OK, Ruth?"

I nodded. Agent Dan took a camera out of his jacket pocket, pointed it at me, and was done before I could even smooth out my sweatshirt.

"You did great, Ruth," Agent Shivani said, patting my leg.

I kept my eyes averted, looking at the weave of the jeans. *Of course I did,* I thought. *Ruth doesn't ever make trouble or break the rules.*

six

OUR FIRST NIGHT in the village, as I lay on the cot in the bunkhouse sweating in the summer heat, my parents had a whispered conversation about what staying would mean. Mom wasn't saying much. Dad had made the choice for all of us.

"We're not going back to Montana," he whispered. "There's nothing for us there."

I slit my eyes open, trying to see my mother's reaction, but her back was all I could see. From the way she was sitting on her cot, slumped forward with her shoulders raised, she appeared to have lost her head.

I waited for her to say something, to tell Dad that I had a life back there. But she remained silent. Before Eric got sick, she used to fight for me. When Dad refused to let me go trick-or-treating on my own with my best friend Chelsea, Mom said I could go. She would buy me lip gloss even when Dad disapproved. But when my brother got sick, I became invisible to both of them. Even after he was gone, they still didn't see me.

I sat up on the cot, my legs dangling over the side, not quite reaching the floor.

"Why don't I get a say?" I asked.

Dad turned to look at me.

"Go to sleep," Dad said. "This is an adult discussion."

"I'm not a baby. I'm almost nine." I looked at Mom, but she was looking at the floor.

"Let's get some air," Dad said, taking Mom's hand and leading her to the door.

I leapt off my cot and starting shoving my feet into my shoes. "I'm coming too!"

"Get back in that bed, Zoe," Dad said over his shoulder. I could hear the mad in his voice.

"But—"

"Go to sleep. Now." He pushed Mom out the door and he followed.

I crossed my arms in front of me and grunted. I threw myself back and turned over on my cot with its lumpy pillow and tried to fall asleep. I was so angry and my heart hurt. Eventually I drifted into fitful dreams. When I woke in the morning, my dad was humming while boiling water for his coffee.

"Good morning!" he sang. "Big day today."

I rubbed the sleep from my eyes and squinted at the light pouring through the window from the shared kitchenette at the front end of the bunkhouse.

"Why?" I asked.

"Hmm? Why what?" Dad said.

"Why is today a big day?"

Dad smiled at me as he handed me a glass of milk, then stirred his instant coffee in a mug.

"I can't tell you yet. Wait until your mother is up."

When my mother rolled off her cot, she stretched her arms above her head. "That was the best sleep I've had in a year," she said. She glided toward my father and took the steaming mug from his hands. "How did you sleep?"

"Grand," Dad said, leaning down to kiss Mom on the lips. "Now that the decision is made, I feel I can rest."

As I drained my glass, I stood in between my parents, like the point of a triangle. I waited for them to say something more, to tell me what was going on. They just stared at each other, a secret message passing between them. I shifted from one foot to the other, hoping my movement would remind them I was right there, waiting. I cleared my throat. I sighed, loudly.

"Why's it a big day?" I repeated.

My parents looked at me like they had something to tell me and weren't sure how I was going to take it. It was the same look they gave me when they told me about my brother's cancer.

"We've decided to stay here," Dad said. "We're going to be moving to our own trailer later this afternoon."

I let my eyes travel to my mother. I expected her to be looking at the ground, but she was looking straight at me, a light of hope in her eyes. She wanted this too.

"Do I get a vote?" I asked, hoping the good sleep changed things from last night.

Dad shook his head. "Sorry, sweetie. Not about this. This is our life now. It will be made official tonight in the naming ceremony."

Tears sprang to my eyes. "What if I don't want this life?" I whined. "Why can't we go back to Montana? I want to see my friends. I was perfectly happy in that life."

My father was already walking away from me. My mother's body was turned half between me and Dad.

"Please," I begged, "I don't want to live here."

I knew which way she was going to go even before she turned her back on me.

I made myself some scrambled eggs for breakfast, but by the time I put them on my plate, I had lost my appetite. I pushed the glistening eggs around the plate until they were cold.

"Get dressed," my mother ordered as she went into the bathroom. "We're going to meet the others."

Others, who? I wondered. "I'm not going," I grunted, crossing my arms over my chest. I had no intention of moving.

"I don't care if I have to drag you out of here in your nightgown," my father snarled. "You *are* coming and you *will* behave."

I looked over defiantly at Dad. I was ready for a fight. My dad glared at me. I held his gaze, not willing to back off. I didn't care how much trouble I would be in. The only way I was going to get off my chair was if we were leaving to go home.

Dad's jaw loosened, and he broke our staring contest. He came over to the table and crouched beside me.

"I know this is hard," he murmured, "but we need to do this. Your mom and I … we just want to be happy. Don't you want us to be happy? Hasn't this family had enough sadness?"

His words hit me like a punch in the stomach. He was right. I was tired of being sad most of the time. It would be good to laugh again, to feel the air under my feet like I did when Eric used to push me on the swings. I nodded and shuffled over to my bunk and put on the sweatshirt and sweatpants I had thrown on the floor last night.

As we toured the compound, I noticed my mother was walking lighter, almost bouncing around. My father continued his humming while we were shown where things were. The school trailer, the infirmary, the gardens. The indoor and outdoor kitchens. We walked for hours, as people waved to us and stopped what they were doing to shake my parents' hands or give them hugs and smile down at me. Every woman wore the same dress; the men wore similar pants and shirts.

"It's a blessed day for your family."

"Tonight, things will get better."

"I remember our naming day like it was yesterday."

I walked around trapped inside my own head. I worked to keep the rolling bubbles in my stomach from climbing up and out my throat. For the whole day, I felt like I was outside my body, watching the activity from above the village.

At dusk, my parents were called into the gathering trailer to meet with Abraham, the man who apparently ran this whole place, his wife, and some other people. Left on my own, I wandered to the other side of the trailer and watched three women at a firepit. They were piling wood, making neat stacks that looked like little log cabins. Two more women joined them, pulling something behind them. They were walking toward me and one of them smiled and waved. I lifted my hand slowly in response but stopped waving when they came around the edge of the firepit. They were dragging the duffel bags my parents had brought with us from Montana and my pink and yellow suitcase. They placed them beside the wood piles.

"Why do you have my suitcase?" I called out.

The women exchanged glances before one of them, a woman in the ugliest brown dress I had ever seen, answered. "It's part of the ceremony, dear girl," she said.

"What are you going to do with our stuff?"

Before they could tell me, I heard the door to the gathering trailer squeal open. My parents stepped out and were hugging the others. Dad brought a hand to his face and I'm sure I saw him wipe away tears. Mom was looking around and when she spotted me, she gestured for me to come.

"This is going to be good for all of us, I promise," my mother whispered in my ear as she wrapped me in a hug. "Things will be very different now."

"OK," was all I could say. I had shared so few words with my parents once my brother got sick. Anytime I had tried to talk to them or give them a detailed answer to a question, they drifted off. Sometimes they walked away from me when I was in the middle of a sentence. Sometimes they nodded or laughed at the wrong times in my story.

We walked back to the firepit, taking a seat on a wooden bench that hadn't been there a moment ago. My mother draped her arm over my shoulders, and I leaned into her warmth. When

I looked up at her, she looked back, then kissed the top of my head.

Others drifted in, forming a circle around us and the pit. One of the women who had been piling the wood outside the pit now arranged logs inside it. The logs leaned against each other, forming a triangle. Placing what looked like a ball of lint in the center, she lit a match and within seconds, a small fire burned. Another woman added small twigs and dead leaves. The fire grew, licking its way around the propped-up logs. My nose filled with the scent of campfire, smoky and sweet.

One by one, other people picked up a log and added it to the fire. I listened to the pop and sizzle of the wood. I watched the flames rise higher, burning above my head. Abraham stepped into the light, his black hair shining and skin glowing orange in the pillar of flames. He walked around the fire, arms open wide. I really wanted to hate him, this man who played a part in making us stay, but there was nothing mean about him. His smile spread across his round face and when his eyes caught mine, I saw nothing but warmth in them. He saw me, and it felt good.

"How fortunate we are to have another family join us," he announced. "It is a testament to the harsh and troubling changes in the world beyond our village. We welcome you, offer you shelter from your pain, and provide hope for the new future."

I looked across the fire, trying to see faces. As the flames flicked at the sky, I caught glimpses of the other people who lived here. Their eyes were closed, and their lips were curled into smiles. Hands clasped together in prayer. Heads nodding.

"Tonight," he thundered, "you will find yourself among a new family with new names. From here, we scrub off what you were and focus on what you will become."

Abraham reached down, opened my suitcase, and upended its contents over the flames. Everything I loved—my favorite books, the best blue jeans and shorts and T-shirts I'd ever owned, were swallowed by fire. The photo of my best friend, Chelsea, and I, smoked before curling into a ball. The stuffed lion that Eric gave me, the one he said would protect me when he was gone, was melting into a heated stink of fake fur and cotton stuffing. I tried to lunge forward, to save what I could, but my mother's arm was pressed down on my shoulders, physically preventing me from doing so. As my things shriveled into the ashes, my heart withered and tears streamed silently down my face.

The process was repeated with the few items my parents had brought with them from Montana. Everything from our past went up in flames.

"From today forward, you shall be called Reuben." Abraham turned from the flames and addressed my father. "Your wife is now Diana. And your child"—he turned to me, cupping my chin —"shall from here on be called Ruth."

Ruth. I turned the name over in my mind. I'd never met a Ruth before. It seemed like an old-lady name.

Abraham clapped once and everyone in the circle held hands. They started singing an unfamiliar song, but in it I heard our new names being called.

After the naming, there was wine for the adults and apple cider for the kids. As the night grew darker and the adults were stumbling and laughing loudly, the fire continued to burn high and hot. People sang and danced, not always well. More than once, someone stumbled too close to the fire but was pulled to safety at the last second. Well into the night, people came one after another to hug and congratulate me.

My parents laughed and smiled the whole night. I stood off to the side, watching them in conversation with other patrons. Every now and then, Mom or Dad would look at me, and I no longer saw the lines carved into the corners of their eyes or their foreheads. My mother blew me a kiss. My father gave me a thumbs-up.

I wandered back to the firepit, watching the weakening flames. I scanned the edges of the ashes, looking for remnants of my things. There was nothing but glowing charcoal.

"Marshmallow?" a voice said.

I hadn't noticed the girl step up beside me. She held out a roasting stick with a jumbo marshmallow speared on its end. Her strawberry-blond hair hung past her shoulders, blowing in the gentle breeze. Her skin was pale, but not sick-looking like my brother's. Because of the dying fire, her eyes looked almost black.

"You want one?"

I shook my head.

"Are you sure? They're really good." She waved the marshmallow so close to my face, I could smell the sugar.

Again, I shook my head. She shrugged her shoulders and sat on the wooden bench, holding the stick just above the dying flames. Other kids emerged out of the darkness, sitting to roast their own marshmallows.

I stood rooted to the spot, horrified. These kids were browning their treats over the embers of my life.

"Can you just not?" I yelled, my face hot with indignation. "How can you eat those after all my things were burned in there?"

All the chattering around the fire stopped. A girl with white-blond hair and bright blue eyes glanced at the others before she leaned closer to me and whispered, "We don't talk about before, ever. No one does, Ruth. Not even in private."

I looked at the others. No one was looking back at me.

"Before doesn't matter," a boy with messy brown hair muttered. He stared into the fire, as did the redheaded boy next to him. The light from the flames danced in their eyes. "Trust me … trust us, Ruth. It's better if we never, ever talk about that."

I wanted to talk about what life was like in Montana and why we had come, but everyone fell silent, so I just nodded. The blond girl shuffled her feet in the sand around the firepit. The boy with the messy hair poked at the smoking logs with a stick. The other two watched the flames.

"I'm Hannah, by the way," said the girl who first offered me a marshmallow. "That's Abigail." She pointed to the blond, then the redhead. "That's Noah, and that guy with the messy curls is James. How old are you?"

"Eight," I answered, leaning forward and huddling my knees. I focused on the embers, watching the shades of orange, yellow, and red flicker through.

"So am I," Hannah said. "Abby and Noah too. James is already nine."

"Have you seen the playground?" Abigail asked. I shook my head.

Noah jumped up. "Let's go, then!"

"Right now? Isn't it too late?"

"That's what makes it fun." Hannah snickered.

The playground, next to the school trailer, was shrouded in darkness. I could see the outline of the climbing structure in the hard blackness of night, with only the glow of the moon lighting the way.

"We call the swings!" Hannah shouted, grabbing my hand and pulling me to the two seats dangling from chains. As we rocked our bodies and pumped our legs, I felt lighter. I was laughing, and I squealed when James came up behind me and gave me a push, launching me higher. With every rise into the air, I forgot the reasons I wanted to leave. A new name, a new life, and new friends, none of who looked at me with pity in their eyes. No one knew me as the girl who'd lost her brother. Maybe it wouldn't be so bad.

When I couldn't swing anymore, I jumped off, and Hannah did the same.

"I'm really tired," I said. "I think I'm going to go."

"Do you know which trailer is yours?" Hannah asked.

I shook my head. I had no idea where to go.

"We'll find out," James said. He took Noah and Abigail with him.

I sat on the end of the slide. Despite the cool night air, the metal was still warm. Hannah squeezed in next to me.

"Are you OK?" she asked.

I didn't know what to say. I was feeling so many things.

"This is a good place to live," Hannah said. "There are a lot of rules, but it makes me feel … kinda safe. I know what I can and can't do. What I'm supposed to do. You'll probably get your chore list tomorrow. I hope you get the garden assignment and then you can pull weeds with me."

I kicked at the gravel under my shoes. That did not sound fun at all.

"Found your trailer!" James called out from the dark. He was alone now. "Come on. I'll show you."

We walked toward the village, where most of the trailers were. They were lined up side by side, separated by large grassy areas and short unpainted fences.

"This is yours," James said, stopping in front of a long, beige trailer. The aqua-blue stripe painted across the middle was flaking, but otherwise, it looked almost new. Light spilled from the windows.

"I'll come find you tomorrow," Hannah said. "I'm really glad you're here." She wrapped her arms around me, squeezing me in a short hug. "Good night."

"Good night," I echoed. James gave me a thumbs-up. I

watched them walk away, chatting and laughing. My heart ached for my best friend. I hadn't even been allowed to say goodbye to Chelsea before we left.

Perched on the bottom step, I opened the trailer door. My nose tingled from the sharp scent of pine cleaner. I stepped inside, right into the kitchen. To my left, at the front, was a living room. To my right, a hallway stretched to the rear, ending at a bedroom. I walked down, opening a door to the bathroom and then a second door on the opposite side to a smaller bedroom.

My parents were not yet back from their own celebration, but neat piles of clothing had been laid out on the bed of the smaller bedroom. I moved them all to the couch, brushed my teeth, and got into a nightgown pulled from the pile. I climbed into bed, not caring that I rolled into the dip in the middle of the mattress. I let the warmth of the whole night lull me to sleep. It felt so good to feel whole again, to be known only as Ruth, the new girl. I slept deeply that night and didn't even hear my parents come in.

seven

THE FOLLOWING MORNING, my parents were using my new name, as if they were feeling how it rolled off their tongues.

"How did you sleep, Ruth?"

"Did you make any new friends last night, Ruth?"

"Ruth, can you put the kettle on to boil, please?"

For the first time since my brother got sick and died, they noticed me. But not me, really. I—Zoe—was erased and in my place was Ruth.

We were dressed and ready for the day when a group of three women knocked on the trailer door. They came bearing loaves of bread, a bowl of salt, and a small pail of honey. They introduced themselves as Mara, Leah, and Naomi.

"Bread so you will never go hungry, salt to connect you to the earth, and honey for a sweet life," Mara explained. My parents invited them in, and we tore a loaf apart, drizzled salt and honey on our hunks, and sank our teeth in. I had never tasted honey and salt together before, and it was a surprise. The honey spread over my tongue, the salt made my mouth water, and the bread was the perfect texture to combine both sensations.

"This is *so good*," I exclaimed.

Naomi laughed and said, "The honey comes from our own bees, Ruth, and of course we bake the bread too. I'll take you out to the apiary one day."

"The what?" I asked, my mouth stuffed.

"The bee farm. Where the hives are, where the honey comes from." She smiled.

"I once climbed a tree to get fresh honey from a beehive!" I exclaimed. "It was worth all the scrapes and cuts I got from the bark. I didn't even get stung once."

"Well, we don't need to be climbing any trees here," Mara said, pursing her lips like she'd sucked a lemon.

"I can assure you Ruth will not be doing anything like that," my mother said.

"Why not? Aren't there any trees here?" I asked just before I shoved another piece of bread into my mouth.

"Abraham says we must never dishonor what nature has given us," Naomi said. "And we must never dishonor Abraham."

The way she said it made me stop chewing. All three women were glaring at me, like I had done something wrong. I was nervous but didn't know why.

"But—"

"Thank you for the wonderful welcome," my father said, cutting me off. "We are so very happy to be here."

Dad scowled at me after he closed the door behind them, but I wasn't sure why. I took the spoon from the honey pot and stuck it in my mouth. A feeling of loss came over me. I missed my brother badly.

"I wonder what Eric's new name would have been," I mused aloud.

My mother dropped the shallow bowl of salt she was about to move to the counter and hissed, "Why would you say that?"

My eyes burned with tears. This was going to be bad.

"I … I don't … I was just thinking about him," I stuttered. "I … I miss him sometimes."

My father stormed away from us, marching out of the trailer. My mother grabbed a towel from the small kitchen and swept the salt off the edge of the table and back into the bowl.

"Why ... did ... you ... say ... that?" she repeated, each word punctuated with the whoosh of the towel.

Salt flew everywhere. I knew I'd be finding it with my bare feet for the next few days. I started scooping salt into a pile, wanting to be helpful, hoping things would be OK again.

"Why? That part of our lives is over, Zo—" She stopped herself. She shook her head and continued sweeping the table, even though the salt was cleared. I could see in her eyes that she was gone for me now.

I slipped into my shoes and walked out of the trailer. I went looking for my father, but he wasn't in the garden or the outdoor kitchen. I poked my head into the gathering trailer, but it was empty. By the time I returned to our own trailer, the chill of the morning had been replaced with the rising heat of the day. Dad wasn't back and now Mom was gone too. The remnants of my family had scattered like the grains of salt.

This had been all my fault. I should have kept my mouth shut and not wrecked everything. Last night, I witnessed a side of my parents I hadn't seen in a long time. Their sadness was gone. And in that moment, standing alone in the trailer that was to be our new home, I knew what I had to do.

If being Ruth was going to make my parents happy again, I was going to be the best Ruth ever.

eight

THE SECOND NIGHT in the hospital, I tossed and turned the whole time, the mattress crinkling with every movement. The sheet under me slid and bunched. I lay in the semidarkness, listening to the quiet conversations of the night nurses in the hall and the random beeping of machines. I was thirsty, but I didn't want to bother anyone. Fortunately, my room had its own bathroom. I rolled off the mattress and padded in, turned on the cold tap, and stuck my mouth under the stream.

I crept back to my bed and tried again, fruitlessly, to will myself to sleep. Morning announced itself with the whoosh of the door and the curtain flying open. A woman shuffled in, pushing a buggy filled with vials, gauze, and bandages.

"Good morning," she chirped. "I'm here to take some blood."

I remained silent, watching her fill two vials. I compressed the cotton ball she placed over the needle hole as she labeled my blood.

"I hope you can get back to sleep," she said, sticking a bandage over the cotton.

When she left, I turned on the wall-mounted TV in my room, muting the volume as I flipped from channel to channel. Nothing was familiar. Television was a privilege reserved for Abraham's special crew, my dad among them. Late at night, when they thought I was sleeping, Dad would tell Mom about some of the things he had seen: footage of a lone gunman holing up in a high-rise hotel randomly firing into a concert crowd, mass shootings in schools, suicide bombers, mad drivers running down tourists on bridges.

"The apocalypse is coming at the hands of our fellow human beings," I heard him say. "Abraham is worried the madness of the world is coming for us."

I didn't understand what it all meant, but the worry in his voice was enough to scare me.

On my second round through the fourteen available channels, I stopped when I saw an overhead view of blackened fields. The next image was that of the charred ruins of the schoolhouse trailer right next to what I recognized as the burnt-out playground. I sat up in bed too quickly, sending the remote flying across the room. I watched myself walk to the ambulance, my face blurred out, my dress stained with filth. The bottom of the screen read "Girl recovered from commune is believed to be the only survivor."

Abraham's photo appeared, and I jumped out of bed to get the remote so I could hear what the newscaster was saying. I winced as pain shot through my ankle, but steadied myself. By the time I managed to turn up the volume, all I caught was *"Investigation is ongoing, with authorities sifting through the wreckage. More on the news tonight at six."*

I glanced at the clock on the wall above the sliding door, the red numbers glowing 6:23. I didn't know if I'd still be here for the next update. For now, I turned off the TV and climbed back into bed. I lay on my side, hugging my knees to my chest, and pulled the covers over my head. This had to be a dream. Maybe I could disappear and magically be transported back to the village. I followed the rules. I did what I was told. Why did this happen to me? Bad things didn't happen to me, to Ruth. I wanted to wake up under the chicken coop and have everything be back to the way it was.

I'm not sure how long I lay there, the light seeping through the thin hospital blankets. I listened to the soft footsteps of the nurses walking past. Carts on wheels rolled from room to room. It was impossible to sleep with all this activity. I wondered how anyone ever got better with all these disruptions.

"Ruth, are you awake?"

I pulled the covers off my head. Dr. DiPaolo stood there, stethoscope draped around her neck, hands holding on to both sides of the tubing.

"How are you feeling?"

"OK." I was not OK. Not at all. I just wanted to make things easier for everyone. Not cause problems. Not ask for anything.

"That's good," she said, walking over to the bed, picking up my wrist to check my pulse. "I don't know if anyone told you, but there is a press conference in about thirty minutes."

"A what?"

"The media—television, newspapers—they want to know what happened. They want to know how you are doing."

I swallowed the lump lodged in my throat. "Do I have to talk to them?"

Dr. DiPaolo shook her head. "No, but—"

"Hey, can I come in?" It was Gary, pushing aside the curtain covering the now-open sliding glass door.

I nodded, hoping he was about to tell me there wouldn't be a press conference.

"Hey, Ruth." He smiled. "How are you feeling?"

"OK," I said for the second time, still not OK. I was tired. I was scared. I wanted my mom. I wanted my old life.

He looked over at the doctor. "Did you tell her about the press conference?"

She nodded and turned back to me, pressing the stethoscope to my chest.

"You don't need to be there," Gary said. "I actually think it's best if you stay here in your room. Dr. DiPaolo will answer any questions about your medical status. I'll be taking questions about what's next for you."

"What *is* next for me?"

"I don't know." Gary shrugged. "But we're going to start by trying to find your grandmother."

When I was alone again, I turned the television back on. I kept pressing the buttons, moving from one channel to the next. On a third pass, I stumbled on Gary and Dr. DiPaolo sitting at a long table, a microphone in front of each of them. The press conference was already underway. Words stuttered into my headspace.

Stable. Minor injuries. Scratches. Trauma.

Assessment. Safe. Family. Home.

I heard Gary call me Jane Doe, and then reporters fired questions all at once.

"Does she know why they were killed?"

"Did she know that something was coming?"

"Will she be able to live a normal life?"

I didn't know the answers to any of their questions and neither did Gary nor the doctor. What I did know was that we moved to the village because my dad said he wanted to live somewhere where life was simple and structured and pain-free.

I continued to watch, a knot twisting inside me. I heard a reporter call my village a "cult" and another ask if the fire was deliberately set. I clenched my teeth, trying to hold in my outrage.

The knot twisted tighter. My body went stiff, and I couldn't move. Every part of me went cold.

As Agents Dan and Shivani took seats at the table to answer questions, I replayed everything I knew about that night. The violence of the gunshots. The enormity of the fire. The crying and the screaming. That sickly smell in the smoke. It was a horror I would have to live with forever.

"Can you tell us who the shooter was?" an unseen voice asked.

"We are still investigating," Agent Dan answered.

"Was this a murder-suicide?" a different voice shouted.

Agent Shivani looked directly into the camera. "We can't comment on that right now. Anything is speculation at this point."

"Does the girl know she is the only one still alive?"

Gary nodded. "She does, and we are doing everything we can to help her through this trauma."

I watched the faces of the only four people who made up my world right now. They were looking at each other, realizing no one had taken the time to explain what it meant to be the lone survivor of what the TV people were calling the Idaho Massacre.

My parents were dead. My brother was dead. My friends were dead. The person Abraham had helped me become over the last seven years was erased, and now I had no idea who I was supposed to be.

nine

AFTER THE PRESS CONFERENCE, Gary stuck to me like gum on a shoe. He didn't say much, but neither did I.

"Do you want to talk about anything?" he asked every time he came to check on me.

Each time, I shook my head. "Not right now, thanks," was my stock answer. Each time, a door inside me slid closed, one after another, shutting my pain away. Silence was the better option. Maybe if I never told anyone that my parents ripped me away from my old life and changed all our names at the commune, the pain could be locked away forever.

I spent the rest of the morning and afternoon pacing the halls in the short-stay unit, proving to the nurses that my legs and ankle could hold me. Over the course of the day, I watched other patients come and go, their families meeting them to take them home.

When Dr. DiPaolo discharged me from the hospital that evening, I was placed in temporary care in the three-story group home Gary ran in Idaho Falls. He told me it wasn't a foster home, but a stop on the way to the next place you would live. I didn't really talk to the other kids on the first day, but not because I didn't want to. I was drifting, like a ghost stuck in limbo between this world and the one that had burned to the ground.

It didn't help that people with camera lenses as long as my arm lurked across the street, trying to catch me walking by a window or out in the yard. Lucky for me, I didn't have to go anywhere because I didn't have anywhere to go.

The bedroom I was assigned on the second floor was sparse. There was a single bed, a three-drawer dresser, and an armless chair upholstered with gold-flecked velvet so worn down I could almost see the frame. A small round mirror, barely bigger than my head, was the only thing hanging on the walls. Nothing in the room matched. The single window was covered with heavy-duty blackout curtains. I pulled them open, taking in the view of the backyard and the garbage bins lined up along the gravel lane. When I sat on the bed, it sagged, forcing me to lean into the middle. The bedspread was a soft gray chenille covered in embroidered gerbera daisies. It was the only pretty thing in the room.

When I ran my hand over the silky threaded petals of a purple bloom, tears sprang to my eyes. Purple was my favorite color. Mom had surprised me one year by planting purple daisies in our garden. After they bloomed, Mom showed me how to tend to them by pinching off the spent flowers to make room for new buds. Even now, after I had lost everyone and everything, the memory of that deep rich tone in our garden was a comfort.

I lay back on the bed, closing my eyes. My mind was flooded with images of the burnt-out trailers and the blackened fields in the village. The screams and shrieks came back, filling empty spaces inside me. I covered my ears, trying to block out the sound of the tortured cries of my friends and family. *The mind is your most powerful tool*, Abraham often reminded us. *Use it to control yourself and make good choices.*

I forced myself to wipe those visions away, replacing them with better memories of swimming in the river with my friends and baking scones with Mom. I rubbed my cheeks, imagining I could feel the weight of Dad's arms resting on my own when he taught me how to chop wood.

I threw myself back on my pillow. *Whose mind was in control when the decision was made that everyone should die?*

A soft knock at the door stopped me from digging any deeper. I pushed myself off the bed and yanked the door open.

"Yes?" I murmured.

"How's it going?" Gary asked me, his eyes searching mine.

"It's not exactly a paradise," I muttered. My face flushed and I clapped my hands to my mouth. I hadn't meant to say that out loud. I looked down at my feet and clenched my eyes shut, waiting for reprimand.

"Come on. That's a little harsh. That velvet chair is opulent décor … for 1885."

I looked up at him, ready to apologize, but he was smiling at me.

"I guess it's better than being under a chicken coop." I sighed.

Gary laughed, and I stood a bit taller. I felt a little lighter, like I could be a different me here. I hadn't felt like this for a long time. Maybe my big mouth could make people laugh again instead of getting me into trouble.

"How long will I be here?"

"I have no clue, Ruth. We're still trying to find your grandmother."

"Maybe she's dead too," I said. The space between Gary's eyebrows scrunched together. I returned the look with my own lifted eyebrows.

"What?" I shrugged. "She was already old to me the last time I saw her."

Gary shook his head. "Not everyone you know is dead."

"But everyone I love is."

He opened his mouth and closed it again, like a fish. There was nothing he could say to dispute that fact.

"Can I interest you in a hot chocolate?" he asked. "It's the only thing I make well."

I nodded, following him down to the kitchen. The other kids in the house drifted in and out of view, waving timidly, nodding slightly, or ignoring me completely. That was OK with me. I wanted to be invisible again, blending into the background.

I sat quietly at the kitchen table, savoring the sweet, hot drink. For the first time in as long as I could remember, I had nothing to do. My hands were idle and there was nobody to assign me any chores. I would have thought this would be a welcome change, but without chores, what was my purpose? *Work anchors us to our community*, Mom said. I knew what she meant. Some of the best and deepest conversations with Hannah happened when I was done my own chores and sauntered over to help her hang laundry on the lines.

"This is really good," I said to Gary as he settled into the chair across from me. "Thanks."

"I'm glad you like it. The best way to make it is to use both milk and water with the chocolate."

With each sip, warmth flooded me, as if the rich cocoa was lifting the loneliness.

"Why does hot chocolate make someone feel better?" I asked.

"All the little chocolate atoms hugging your insides," Gary answered. I rolled my eyes, but Gary didn't notice.

He was flipping the pages of a newspaper, the words from the headlines blurring by. *Shocking. Tragic. Explosion. Shopping mall. National. President. Government. Conspiracy.* The words were disturbing. Maybe my dad had made the right choice, protecting us in the bubble of the commune. Maybe Abraham was right. Life outside was dangerous.

My right leg started jittering under the table. I rested my

hand on my thigh to still the outside while I tried to calm my inside.

When my mug was empty, I walked over to the sink to wash it. It was a colossal mistake. As soon as I looked out the picture window, the action started. At first it was two photographers and then the rest must have caught on because they were running into the open yard at the back of the house, cameras pointed toward me.

"Umm, Gary … photographers are on the property."

Gary pushed his chair back with a screech. He ran up behind me and gently nudged me away from the window.

"You might want to consider getting a fence," I said as I walked toward the stairs, heading to my new bedroom.

ten

"DO you think someone would try to kidnap me?"

Gary started to shake his head and then stopped. "I'm not sure, Ruth. Events like this bring out the best and worst in people. I don't want to freak you out, but just be aware of who is around you."

Two days after I moved into Gary's "halfway house"—we were all halfway to somewhere else, after all—the police forced the media to the end of the street. There were barricades at both ends that had to be moved anytime the neighbors wanted to leave their own homes. A group of them came to the door with their complaints. While I hid in my room, leaning my ear against the door to listen, I heard them telling Gary I needed to go somewhere else.

"We pay our taxes," a man said in a raised voice. "We have the right to come and go as we please. You need to fix this, Gary, or we will make a formal complaint to the city and shut this place down."

The anger didn't stop at the front stoop. Inside these walls, the other kids were angry too.

"We can't go anywhere without reporters shoving microphones in our faces asking about Ruth," I heard Alex, a boy who had been at the house for a month, say.

"Can't you just kick her out?" I heard a girl whine.

"No, Fanta, I won't kick her out," Gary said, "any more than I would put any of you out. It's my duty to protect everyone in this house, and I take that very seriously. Would any of you have wanted that for yourselves shortly after you arrived?" No one answered him.

By the end of my first week, strangers started knocking on the door. There were a lot of people in the world who wanted to help "the Idaho Massacre girl," dropping off bags and boxes in front of the house. When the first bag labeled "For Ruth" appeared, Gary called the police, telling them a suspicious package had been delivered.

"Suspicious? Why?" I asked no one in particular.

"People leave bombs in bags," said Jasmine, an angry waif who had arrived at the home a week before me.

"Why would anyone do that?"

Her cobalt eyes swept over me from my bare feet to my stringy hair. Even though she was almost two years younger than me, I cringed under her scrutiny.

"Crazy doesn't need a reason," she sneered. "Haven't you figured that out by now, cult girl?"

I fled to my bedroom, the only place in the house where I could be alone. I slid against the closed door, wondering if I was ever going to be free of the commune or if I would now live my whole life as "cult girl." I had visions of another round of insanity coming on the heels of the arrival of police, firefighters, bomb squad, and FBI.

Forty-five minutes after Gary made the call, two police officers showed up in their cruiser. I went down to the living room, curiosity pulling me away from my grief. Through the front window, I could see the officers already looked bored. One approached the bag using a long metal rod with pincers on the end. It seemed stupid to me for them to think that was going to provide enough distance in case a bomb was hidden inside the black plastic trash bag. I pressed my face sideways against the glass, trying to see what they were doing.

"You need to get away from the window," Gary said, pulling me into the safety of the kitchen. "Not a smart place to be right now."

When a knock came at the door about fifteen minutes later, Gary opened it to see one of the police officers standing there with the bag opened. I walked up behind Gary and peered around him. There *was* an explosion in that bag—an explosion of clothes and shoes.

"Nothing harmful in here," the officer told us. "But this …" He reached into the bag and pulled out a sweater covered in plastic, jewel-like beads of many colors. "This should be labeled a criminal offence." He wasn't wrong. He laughed at his own joke and Gary joined him.

"Thanks for coming, Officer," Gary said, reaching for the bag. "I feel silly having called."

The officer waved the grabber in the air like a wand. "No need. You did the right thing. Better safe than sorry." The officer walked back to his car, his partner already behind the wheel. "Don't hesitate to contact us if it happens again," he called out.

We brought the bag into the living room and dumped the contents onto the hardwood floor. I sat cross-legged in front of the pile and pulled things out. The variety was shocking. There were shoes, pajamas, dresses, and pants. Two packages of new underwear with six pairs in each. I was never going to have to wear the same dress as everyone else ever again. In the discard pile went the bejeweled sweater, a pair of shoes whose bottoms had separated from the top, and anything ripped or stained. The clothes that were for boys or were way too small or big for me went into another pile for the other kids in the house.

"That's a good haul," Gary said, examining the clothing in front of me. There was enough to get me through at least two weeks without doing any laundry.

"I can't believe people would just give me this stuff. For free."

"There are a lot of caring people in this world. Try to remember that when you think life is being unkind and unfair. Not everyone wants to hurt you."

"Yeah, well, I'm not convinced that's true. Too many people get to make choices for me, whether I like it or not."

I held my breath, waiting for a lecture on ingratitude, selfishness, and respect. I was used to paying a price for any random thought that made its way from my brain to my mouth. Abraham would make me come to the front of the dinner hall and tell the community all the ways I was hurting them with my words.

Like Abraham, Gary liked to drop life lessons into our conversations. The difference was it seemed like Gary was OK with me having an opinion and sharing it out loud. I didn't have to apologize endlessly. I didn't have to pretend to be someone I wasn't. In the commune, I had a tight knot in my stomach all the time, like I had eaten a tennis ball. But here, in the halfway house full of lost souls, I felt safer trying out the different versions of me.

During my second week, people started knocking on the door, wanting to convert me to their religion. One aggressive woman tried to yank me out onto the front stoop.

"I shall pull you from the jaws of Satan and help you find your way back to god," she said.

"Everyone I love was killed," I answered, peeling her fingers off my arm, "so don't bring your invisible deities here." I stepped back into the house, gently closing the door.

"I prefer deities that are inclusive of everyone," someone behind me said.

I turned to find Gia smiling behind me, her sage green eyes shining. "Hell never turns anyone away."

A laugh burst out of me, and for a brief second, my sadness

lightened. I slapped my hand over my mouth. "Death is not funny," I said through my fingers.

"Laughter is the only thing that keeps me sane," Gia said. "It takes me away for a moment. Nothing has changed on the outside, but I feel a bit better on the inside. C'mon. Let's get a Coke."

I followed Gia to the back of the house. She opened the door to the basement and started down the stairs. I paused, not sure we were allowed to go there.

"The soda fridge is down here," Gia said when she looked back at me. "Are you scared? Did you get locked in a basement? If you did, I can get—"

"No." I shook my head. "I just … I mean … are we allowed down here?"

Gia grinned. "I've been in enough group homes to know that if they don't want you somewhere, they lock the door. C'mon, weirdo. Get down here."

A smile tugged at my lips. Gia wasn't being mean; the name-calling was a friendly poke. I wanted to ask why she was here, how many homes she had been in and why, but I had been raised to forget the past and never ask questions about someone else's. I kept quiet and followed her down the stairs.

The basement was made entirely of concrete with three washing machines and three dryers along one wall. On the other side were two fridges, as well as floor-to-ceiling shelving stacked full of canned food, bags of pasta and beans, paper goods, and cleaning supplies.

I froze, staring at all the food. A humming started in my head and my eyes stung with tears. Abraham's voice from long ago filled my brain. I had been sick in bed for two days, and he punished me by withholding food for a week.

"What did you do to earn your food? You've done nothing but sit around. If you don't work, then neither shall you eat."

"Ruth? What's happening?"

Gia's voice sounded muffled. I squeezed my eyes closed. I brought my fists to my ears, plugging them. I tried to speak, but my words were lost. I flinched when a cold hand landed between my shoulder blades. It took me a moment to realize it was Gia guiding me up the stairs.

In the living room, I dropped onto the couch. Gia shooed everyone away. She sat next to me, but not so close to be touching any part of me. Her purple-colored hair swung forward as she leaned to peer at my face.

"What's happening?" she repeated. "Who's in your head?"

My hands were on my legs, rubbing up and down my thighs. "Abraham," I whispered.

"The psycho from your commune who killed everyone?"

I gasped. Hearing it out loud made it very real. More than hearing it from Dr. DiPaolo. More than seeing it on the news.

"He's gone," Gia said. "He can't hurt anyone anymore. You're safe."

"Am I?" My voice cracked. "He's still in my head. How do you get rid of that?"

"You can't. You have to find a way to accept that he was crazy to do what he did. People like that get caught up in their own fantasies. No one can crack through. No one would ever dare try."

"How do you know that?"

Gia looked out the living room window. "Because my dad was one of those people, Ruth. He was delusional and ruled our house with an iron fist. He beat the crap out of my mother for some imagined snub. When she finally had the balls to press charges, he killed himself rather than face up to what he did."

I looked at her profile while she continued to gaze. A scar edged her cheek to her chin, thick and blacker than her skin.

"I'm so sorry, Gia. I had no idea."

She shrugged a shoulder. "He did me and my mom a favor. How did you escape?"

"I hid. My mom told me to. I wish I hadn't, though."

Gia turned back to me, nodding her head. "Yeah. These things always end badly."

I picked at the pilled balls on my leggings. "How do you keep going?"

She took my hand in hers, then placed her other hand over mine. "When we lose something, we only look in the dark to find it. But there is so much more to see underneath the light. Turn on your light, Ruth." She squeezed my hand. "Coke?" She picked up one of the cans from the coffee table and handed it to me. "Cheers," she said, tapping her can against mine.

We sat in silence as we drank. Just telling Gia that I'd run had lifted a weight from my shoulders. She didn't judge me; she accepted my choice. Maybe one day I could do that too.

eleven

"ISN'T THERE anything you can do to stop people from coming?" I asked one evening as Gary and I washed the dinner dishes.

"We could build a wall with a guarded gate." Gary smirked. "But my budget is a little too tight for that. Besides, building walls keeps all the good people away too." He looked at me pointedly.

"How long do you think I'll be here?" I changed the subject.

Gary plunged his hands into the soapy water, fishing out a plate to wash. "I don't have the answer to that. I know that family services, the police, and the FBI are doing what they can to find your grandmother."

"What's the longest time a kid ever stayed here?"

"About three months, I think."

"Why so long?"

Gary blew air through his lips, making them flutter. "His family was hard to find. He was a runaway, sixteen years old. He wouldn't tell us where he came from. He had no identification when he came into police custody. He was tight-lipped about everything. It's not unusual to get that from someone who is running away. Sometimes what they've left behind is pretty bad, and they don't want to go back."

"What if they ran away because they were mad about something, like losing TV privileges?"

"Let me ask you something," he said, resting his sudsy hands on the edge of the sink. "Did your parents move you away from everything you knew?"

I nodded.

"So you had to leave your friends, your school, your home, and your routine. They took you to a place where your whole life changed. You were cut off from the outside world. You couldn't call, text, or email anyone. Didn't you ever think about running away?"

"Once. During the first year. But I was eight. Where was I going to go?"

The commune was in the middle of nowhere. I got to the woods at the eastern edge and was too scared to go in. I turned around, walking quickly past the village and across the wheat field. I slowed down as I approached the front gate. It was at least three times my height and made of corrugated metal. There wasn't a single place I could get a foothold on the vertical waves. On either side, barbed-wire fencing extended as far as I could see. I had always assumed the razor-sharp barbs were meant to keep people out. But now I had to wonder if they were supposed to keep us in.

"That's not usually a consideration when someone wants to run. I've known enough runaways to know the escape overrides the destination."

"All I wanted was for things to go back to the way they were," I admitted. "I yelled at my mother, telling her I hated the village, my life, and that I hated her most of all. I gave her the silent treatment. A couple days before the end, we had another fight. I had come home early from school, and she was in my room, going through my old notebooks like she was looking for something. I accused her of spying on me." I blinked back tears, wiping the towel over the surface of the already dry plate. "I was still mad and not talking to her when she told me to run."

Gary laid a hand on mine, stopping me. I pulled my hand away, turning my back on him to put the plate in a cupboard.

"That's a normal part of growing up," Gary assured me. "I don't think there's a person out there who hasn't said something horrible to their parents at one time or another."

Yeah, but did their parents get killed two days later?

"Where did that kid go when he finally left?" I asked, moving the conversation in a different direction.

"He went to live with his older sister …" Gary stopped mid-sentence, perhaps realizing that would never be an option for me.

"Do you ever keep in touch with any of the kids who stay here?"

"If that's what they want, then yes. I am not allowed to reach out to them, but every child leaves here with at least two things —my support and my email."

As we finished up the dishes, I couldn't help but wonder what would happen if my grandmother was never found. Or worse. What if they found her and she didn't want anything to do with me? I wanted to ask Gary what happens to the kids without any family, but I already knew the answer to that. Stories about foster care ran rampant in this halfway house, and none of them were good.

I looked at the ratty and worn dish towel I was holding in my hand, permanently stained and changed, just like me.

twelve

I WOKE up to the smell of French toast and bacon coming from Gary's kitchen. I smiled and then jumped out of bed, throwing on a pair of black leggings and a long-sleeved blue shirt that I'd dug out of one of the trash bags. I raced downstairs, hoping there was something left for me to eat. When I got to the kitchen, a woman was there, flipping the egg-dipped bread on an electric griddle.

She turned as I skidded to a stop on the cold linoleum floor.

"Oh, hey there," she said as she turned to look at me. "I'm Maria. I come here sometimes to cook and clean and help out." Her green eyes traveled up from my feet to the top of my head. I wrapped my arms tight around myself. I'm sure I looked exactly like someone who had just flown out of bed without even dragging a brush through her hair.

"You must be Ruth," Maria said, wiping her hands on a dish towel and extending one toward me. I shook it, but I couldn't take my eyes off her face. Her eyelids were shadowed in shimmering silver and orange. Her eyelashes were thick and black. There was a glow to her, like she was standing in the summer sun, but this was November in Idaho.

"It's not polite to stare." She smiled, her glossed lips breaking into a smile across her perfectly made-up face.

I blinked. "Uh … sorry. I love your makeup. Whatever you did to your eyes … it's amazing. It's like art." I blushed, wishing my mouth would stop moving.

"I can show you how to do this after breakfast if you like. I have some makeup in my bag … hey … are you OK?"

My eyes had flooded and tears spilled down my plain, imperfect face. I used to watch my mother swirling a brush over her eyes, adding a touch of eyeliner, her face stretched out as she applied mascara. She had promised me she would show me what to do when I was old enough. But that was before Eric died and then she stopped wearing any makeup at all.

Maria guided me to the kitchen table and gently pushed me down into a chair. Whenever another kid came into the kitchen, she shooed them into the dining room, her blond ponytail swinging as she tilted her chin.

"I lost my parents in a car accident when I was sixteen," she said, sliding onto the chair next to me, "and it still hurts like crazy. When I turned eighteen a couple of years ago, I spent the whole day in bed wishing my parents were still alive to celebrate this big deal with me. I'm still trying to find ways to not cry every time I see a family spending time together. I will always miss them."

She stood up, walking over to flip the French toast. Then she turned down the heat on a pan of sizzling bacon. She came back to the table and handed me a paper towel. I wiped my face, but fresh tears kept coming.

"Just let it out," she said. "If you try to hold it in, it will be worse." I heard her voice crack and looked up to see her own eyes were a bit wet too.

"Did you … did you live here too?" I sniffed.

She nodded. "I was here for almost a month. My aunt and uncle, whom I went to live with, were traveling in South America when the accident happened. I am still very grateful to Gary for everything he did for me."

"Is that why you come here to cook and stuff?"

"Yep. This house gave me a safe place to grieve and be really pissed off at the same time. I keep coming back because I like to have people around me who won't complain about my cooking. And also to see if there are any other young people who need me to teach them my mad makeup skills." She fluttered her thick lashes. "Good thing we hadn't started yet or your face would be a mess right now."

I stopped crying and a snot bubble came out of my nose as I started to laugh.

"Waterproof mascara will be your friend and savior," she added. "It's hell to get off at night, but can I tell you a secret?" Maria tilted her head to the side to check if anyone was within earshot. "Sometimes, I don't bother taking the mascara off at night so I can have a smoky under-eye thing happening the next day. It makes me feel glamorous."

I laughed again at the thought of Maria's perfectly placed makeup being smudged all over her face.

"OK," she said, clapping her hands. "Let's eat! Can you grab the maple syrup and bring it into the dining room?"

She plated all the food, and I picked up the bottles of maple syrup, not caring that my fingers were getting sticky from the old syrup that had dribbled over the sides. I followed Maria, noticing that the underside of her ponytail was bright blue. I touched my own messy hair, wondering if I could pull off color like that.

"After breakfast, I'll show you how to put on eye shadow. We'll start simple at first. What are you, like, thirteen?"

"I'll be sixteen in January."

"Wow, you've got some good genes. OK, so we don't want to overdo it. The last thing I need is Gary giving me heck because I turned a teenager into a tart. The trick to makeup is knowing when too much is a bad thing and when it's art. Some days you need the drama, and some days you need to be more subtle. Think dance club versus job interview."

Maria had barely placed the food down on the table before

twelve sets of hands were grabbing at the tower of French toast and the heaping plate of bacon. Manners were not enforced here at all. Life in this house was so different from the commune. Eating together was the same, but at the commune, we ate in silence. At Gary's table, multiple conversations happened at the same time. It was loud and lively. Kids swore. They laughed. And Gary encouraged it. No one waited patiently for a platter to be passed around. Gia mouthed "Get in there" as she passed me the bacon. I had missed out on some good food my first week because I didn't realize I was supposed to just dig in.

I watched Maria laugh and listened to her talk to everyone at the table. She never asked anyone why they were here or where they were going. She talked about fun things like video games, comic books, reality TV, and shopping. For thirty minutes that morning, I felt like part of a normal family, not a bunch of kids stuck in between life as it was and life as it was going to be.

thirteen

MY MAKEUP LESSON with Maria was more fun than I expected, especially since Gia asked to join us.

"I hope it's OK," Gia said to me. "I have no idea about any of this." She nudged my shoulder. "Us sheltered girls need all the help we can get."

"That's one way to put it." I smiled. "I've never even tried most of this stuff."

"Same. My dad believed makeup was an abomination."

"Did you think that too?" I asked.

"I didn't know any better to question it, so yeah, I guess I did. What about you?"

"When we moved to the commune, I had only just discovered lip gloss. Not a single woman in the commune wore makeup."

"Well then, I have my work cut out for me," Maria said. She was digging around in her tote bag and pulled out a bulging zippered pouch, about the size of a football. When she opened it, pots and bottles, pencils and brushes, mascaras, and powder fought their way out.

"You young girls with your gorgeous skin." Maria sighed, as she turned my head back and forth, examining me under a desk lamp.

For the next hour, Maria taught us as much as she could about blending, highlighting, and how to not poke our eyes out while putting on mascara. She let us play, laughing along as we deliberately tried to make ourselves look ridiculous with bright colors and excessive blush. We danced and pranced around the house, enjoying the attention and feeling glamorous.

Later, as I scrubbed my face in the shower, the lightness I felt after my morning with Maria and Gia swirled down the drain. Gary had warned me that social services was going to send someone—an exit counselor—to talk to me about my life in the commune. Abraham's warnings about not trusting outsiders drifted into my mind, but so far, everyone I'd encountered had been helpful and kind.

"I'm not crazy," I told the psychiatrist, who introduced herself as Dr. Zaretsky. "I don't believe the earth is flat or anything like that."

She nodded, then wrote something down in the notebook resting on her lap. We were sitting on armchairs in the extension at the back of the house that had been converted into Gary's office.

"What are you writing?" I asked.

When she looked up at me, the side bangs of her hair swung away from her face.

"Does it bother you that I'm taking notes? Do you feel like I'm assessing you?"

"You are. That's your job. To deprogram me."

"Who told you that?"

"I hear the other kids talking." I shrugged.

"Well, Ruth, what you heard is partially right. I'm here to find how how much influence the commune had. I'm not here to judge you, though. I want to know what you think about the world."

I sighed but said nothing. I didn't even know this world. Right now, my world was made up of loss, confusion, loneliness, and fear. The noose of suspicion and mistrust Abraham had wrapped around my neck was only starting to loosen.

"Ruth, it's OK to feel disoriented. You've been through something horrible. You belonged to a close community and now you probably feel unrooted."

I looked out the window behind Gary's desk. When I wiped my eyes, my fingers came away with bits of waterproof black mascara.

"I lost everyone and I don't know how to process that. I knew my place and my role, but now I don't know who I'm supposed to be."

"Let's talk about that. Do you feel you were manipulated to change the way you thought about things?"

"No." I wasn't lying. That was part of the problem. Abraham tried, my parents tried, but I was always fighting back.

"Do you feel disconnected from the world outside the commune?"

"Yes."

"Do you feel you can't trust anyone?"

"I don't know." I looked at Dr. Zaretsky and held her gaze. She blinked twice, the features of her face resting into a neutral zone.

"That's perfectly OK, Ruth. Should we talk about your parents and the commune?"

"What is there to talk about? After my brother died, my parents chose to live in a place where they didn't have to deal with their pain. They were keeping me safe from the horrible things happening in the world. I didn't have a choice other than to blindly accept that."

Something cracked open inside me. I bit my bottom lip, refusing to let the tears loose. For the briefest second, the girl I used to be peered out.

"I'm mad at them for taking me there," I spat. "I'm so pissed off. At them, at Abraham ..." I let the words hang. I took a deep breath, trying to gain control of myself. "I'm sorry … I shouldn't be like that. I should be grateful to be alive."

"Ruth, sometimes we hold a lot of conflicting ideas and feelings at the same time. That's a sign of growth and awareness."

I looked down at my hands. Only two weeks had passed, but already the skin felt softer, and my nails were growing. The rest of me was restless. In the commune, there were always things to do. Laundry to be washed and hung, food to be prepared. A lot of people living together was a lot of work.

"How are you feeling?"

"Can we be done now?" I asked as I turned my head back.

"We still have time," she said, looking at her watch. "Let me ask another way. What are you feeling the most right now?"

Resentment. Fear. Hatred.

"Sad." I sighed. "I never had a chance to say goodbye to anyone. And I can't stand thinking about how they died. If they suffered."

Dr. Zaretsky continued to stare at me, waiting and assessing. Then she nodded to herself and made notes in her book. That must have been the right answer, because she didn't ask for more.

I spent the remainder of the session telling her about the day-to-day life in the commune. I skipped over the parts where I got into trouble for forgetting how to be Ruth.

Dr. Zaretsky came back twice the following week. She was kind and patient, a specialist, she told me, in survivor's guilt. We talked quietly and in short sentences. She said I needed to think about the event differently. As part of my therapy, she lit a match, and panic took over. My legs jittered and I stood from my chair, pacing the room and feeling trapped.

"Instead of seeing the flame as dangerous," she suggested, "view it as a life source." I thought *she* was the crazy one.

"Use your imagination to change the story," she advised. I

was supposed to push away the images in my mind of the burned-out trailers and the screaming and build a new mental album of my friends and family in the before and afterlife, doing things that made them happy.

"It will be a long healing process," she warned. "Give yourself permission to have some very bad days, but remind yourself that what happened is not your fault. Put an image in your head of your mom smiling at you, glad that she told you to run and that you listened."

Every night, as I lay in bed, I worked on remembering only the good things, and with each passing day, I felt more like my old self. One day at a time, the protective layers I had wrapped around myself in the commune loosened. I was laughing again, playing Scrabble with some of the other kids, and I even did a happy dance when I crushed Gary's all-time high score.

At dinner one night, we were celebrating Oscar, who was going home after four days at Gary's. Well, not *home* home but to live with his half brother. Oscar, who was sixteen, ended up here after his mom was put into the hospital. He was the one who found her on the floor in the middle of their living room, lying on her side like she was asleep. She was barely breathing, he told us, and he figured out just in time that she had taken fentanyl.

"I don't know what that is," I said.

"It's pain medicine," Oscar explained. "But it's really potent. Lots of dealers mix it with other drugs because it's addictive."

I'd never known anyone who used drugs or who was related to someone who had. Occasionally in the commune, I heard whispers when someone new came and had to "dry out" for a couple of days, and I understood it had nothing to do with laundry.

"How long will she be in the hospital?"

"This time? Who knows." He shrugged. He twirled spaghetti onto a fork and shoved it into his mouth.

"I'm sorry you have to go through this," I said.

"It's not the first time. It for sure won't be the last. But keep calm and carry on, right?"

I stared at Oscar. I watched his hands—fork in the right, knife in the left—as they moved food from plate to mouth. He had a faint smile on his lips, and I couldn't decide if he was really happy or just faking it.

"Aren't you scared?" I blurted out.

Oscar lifted his face from his plate and tilted his head. "Of what? Her dying? Yes. Of what's going to happen to me? A little. But I'll be OK. What she does is not who I am. I don't care if people judge me for what my mom does."

Oscar turned his face back to his plate, twirling more spaghetti onto the fork.

"How do you do that?" I asked.

"Do what? Twirl spaghetti?"

I shook my head. "How do you brush it off? What people say?"

Oscar shrugged. "Most of the time, they've already decided who I am and how my life will turn out. It's their issue, not mine. You can either let it get in the way, or you can work with what you've got. You're no different from any of us."

Oscar's words ignited a flame inside me. I wanted to grab him by the shirt and shake him.

"You don't know what happened to me," I hissed. "You weren't there. You still have family to go to. Your mother may be a drug addict, but at least she's still alive." I tried to steady my voice, but my pulse was racing. "You know what's next for you. You're not stuck between here and nowhere."

I could feel everyone's eyes on us, watching and waiting. Oscar chewed slowly, his eyes boring into mine.

"Are you serious right now?" he asked.

My rage exploded. "Do you have nightmares of your parents

burning to ashes with bullet holes in their heads? I don't think so. Your whole life hasn't literally gone up in flames."

"Not yet," he answered. "But it could at any time. Same goes for all of us here. Get over yourself, Ruth."

"Don't call me Ruth," I spat. "My name is Zoe."

I pushed away from the table, the legs of my chair screeching on the floor. I ran to my room, slamming the door behind me. I threw myself face down on the bed. My anger dissolved into tears. I screamed into my pillow, pushing out my fury. I was so mad at everyone and everything, but mostly at myself for letting loose. What I had just done was invite a new disaster into my life.

There was a soft knock on my door, and I heard Gary's voice. "Ruth? Can I come in?"

I rolled off the bed and opened the door for him. He held out a box of tissues.

I took it and opened the door fully, inviting him in. I plucked a tissue to wipe my face.

"Really?" I asked, showing him the now-empty box.

He peered into the box, then back at me, raising his eyebrows.

"Maybe I knew you'd only need the one." Gary smirked. "Or maybe I'm just that clueless sometimes."

"My money's on clueless," I snapped, crossing my arms.

"For sure I was clueless about who you are. Care to explain what's going on?"

I tightened my arms across my chest and sighed. Gary and Maria had made me—and all the kids—feel unjudged. Safe. Seen.

So, I chose to level with Gary.

"My name ... my real name ..." I stuttered, my mouth working its way around the truth. "My real name is Zoe Kane. No one has called me that for seven years."

"Well, that changes things, Ru—I mean … Zoe."

"I'm sorry I lied. I lied to everyone who's been trying to help me."

Gary shook his head. "But you didn't. Ruth's been your name for a long time. I get the feeling you know it's not who you really are. And now that we know that," he added, "we'll probably have an easier time finding your grandmother. Are you ready for that?"

It was Ruth who agreed, but inside, Zoe was swirling, trying to claw her way out of a disguise. I pushed Zoe down. The last time I let myself be who I used to be, a boy nearly died.

fourteen

DURING OUR THIRD year in the village, the first snowfall came fast and heavy in early October. When we went to bed, the crisp autumn leaves were clinging to their branches; by morning, the trees were stripped, their leaves buried under more than a foot of snow. Over the course of the day, the snow got fatter and heavier. During recess at school, we stood outside the trailer, catching snowflakes on our tongues, letting the fluffy flakes land on our noses, lips, and lashes. School ended early so we could all pitch in gathering and distributing wood throughout the compound.

For the rest of the day, we worked. Word spread throughout the village that every family should make their way to the community food trailer and stock up on canned goods. We were allowed three cans per person for three days. My mother, father, and I loaded up on canned beans, mushrooms, and soup, with a few cans of chili.

As the storm continued, we hunkered down for the night. Despite the sun dipping behind the mountains, the land brightened, the crusted snow reflected in the light of the moon. The entire compound glowed in crisp whiteness. The wind howled around the trailer, whistling through the metal frame and up through the floor. We turned on our propane heater, bundled in extra clothes and socks, and slept in our hats, scarves, and mittens.

It snowed for two days. By the time it stopped, both my mother and father had to lean against the door of the trailer to push it open. The cold of the air took my breath away, but at the same time, it smelled clean.

Over the course of the day, the sounds built slowly. At first it was the scraping of trailer doors being opened into the snow. Then I heard the grunting and shrieks of other families making their way outside. The laughter of children was next, followed by the roar of our two trucks with plows attached to their fronts, carving paths throughout the village and digging people out of their trailers. It had been cold enough for the river to fully freeze over.

Hannah's dad was one of the people driving a plow. When they got to our trailer, Hannah jumped out of the cab and ran up the newly cut path to our door. "Ruth! Are you up? Ruth?"

I swung open the door and smiled. "Good morning!"

"Come on," she said, tugging my mittened hand. "My dad will drive us over to the river. We're building snowmen."

I couldn't help but get caught up in her excitement. I threw on my parka, grabbed my hat, then ran to the fridge.

"A snowman must have the right nose." I grinned, holding a carrot above my head.

Hannah laughed as we climbed into the back seat of her father's truck.

"Good morning, Ruth." He smiled. "Quite the storm, huh?"

"I haven't seen this much snow in ages. I love it."

"You say that today." He laughed. "But now that you girls are eleven, you're old enough for snow removal. Enjoy the freedom before the work comes." Hannah and I groaned at the same time.

There must have been thirty kids building snowmen in the field by the riverbank. James, Abigail, and Noah were pushing their full weight behind a ball of snow that came up to their knees.

"Hannah, Ruth, come help us!" James called out when he saw us. "We need to make THE BIGGEST SNOWMAN OF ALL TIME!"

Hannah and I looked at each other and grinned. We ran over to our friends, squeezing in between them to help push. As we rolled, Abigail used her mittened hands to pack the snow onto the ball.

"OK, that should be good," Noah said after four rotations. The base of our snowman was now well above our knees. "Let's get to work on the middle section and the head. This is going to be so great!"

For the next two hours, we rolled and packed snow. Just as Abigail and I placed the head on our snowman, something whizzed by my own head and smacked into the back of Abigail's. We whipped around to see Hannah, James, and Noah grinning. James's arm was cocked, a snowball in his gloved hand. He launched, and Abigail and I ducked just in time, squealing with laughter when the snowball hit our snowman square in the face.

We crouched down, making snowballs of our own, throwing them as hard as we could at our opponents. We hid behind the massive form of our snowman, whose head was now above our own.

"SNOWBALL FIGHT!!!" someone yelled.

Chaos erupted. Snow flew in all directions. From the left and right. Behind us and in front of us. From the sky. From the ground as the wind kicked up, swirling white around us all. I laughed so hard, I was crying, the tears freezing at the corners of my eyes and on my lashes. The snow gathered in the folds of my skirt and stuck to the fibers of my scarf, hat, and mittens. After I threw my full weight behind a snowball aimed at Noah, my feet slid out from under me. I lost my balance and tumbled, hooting as I landed on my back.

I lay there, catching my breath, smiling wide. Not caring about the cold seeping through my tights, I listened to the shrieks and peals of laughter all around me. I moved my arms up and down, my legs out and in, making a snow angel in the sticky powder. Hannah flopped down beside me, mimicking my movements to make an angel of her own.

"I haven't had this much fun for a long time," she said, rolling toward me.

I turned my head toward her and grinned. "Me neither," I agreed.

Hannah's eyes locked on mine. "Can I ask you something?" she whispered.

I nodded.

"Are you happy that you came here?"

I looked away, letting the snow fall on my face. I opened my mouth and felt flakes melt on my tongue.

"I thought we're not supposed to talk about that." I bit my bottom lip. Was this some kind of test?

"I'm just curious. I don't remember coming here, and I always wonder what it's like for those who do."

I glanced over. Hannah's light eyelashes glistened with snow.

"I wasn't happy, no," I admitted. "I thought I was being punished."

"Hmmm," was all she said. My mind drifted away, remembering our house and my toys. And Eric. It was hard to believe we'd been here for almost four years. I had already forgotten things from before.

"Do you ever wonder if you could go back?"

I shook my head. "I don't think I could. When I think about how life used to be, I get sad. I felt so alone when my brother got sick. I got mad at him for getting so much attention. For a long time, I thought my brother died because of me. I used to wish he would just die so I could have my parents back."

With her face still to the sky, Hannah reached out a mittened hand and grasped my own, held it. Squeezed it.

"My parents were different people then." I sighed. "I like how we are now. We smile more."

"Ruth, can I tell you something?"

I turned on to my side so we were face-to-face.

"You're my best friend," she said.

Tears sprung to my eyes. My heart was bursting, warming me up from the inside out.

"Same here, Hannah. I …"

I never had a chance to finish my sentence. James, Noah, and Abby, along with some other kids, attacked us with more snowballs than I could count. Even as one pounded me right in the face, I was thinking this was turning into a very good day.

The snow and wind came and went for the rest of the afternoon. After lunch, when I looked out the window of our trailer, the ground sparkled in the sunlight like a million little diamonds. It was beautiful and peaceful and unspoiled. Dad asked me to go to the utility Quonset to find a shovel, since we didn't have one at our trailer.

I didn't like going into the Quonset. Lit by only two pull-string fluorescent lights suspended in the middle of the building, everything inside was shrouded in shadows. It was a terrifying space.

The sliding metal door squealed as I pushed it open. The light from the doorway spilled into the entrance and I looked to my left and my right, hoping to see shovels. No such luck. I was going to have to go deeper.

I shuffled into the darkness, waving my arms out in front of me. I had visions in my head of tripping on a rusty oil can, falling on a rake, and stabbing myself through the eye. I hated this Quonset.

I kept moving forward, shrieking when the string hanging from the lights grazed my face. In the dark belly of the shed, it felt more like hair than cotton. I groped blindly until my hand found the swaying string, then pulled. The lights flickered and buzzed to life.

The area around me and about six feet in front and behind me were now lit, but I couldn't see to the back. If I couldn't find a shovel in the lit radius, I would have to go deeper into the shed, where the spiders and their webs lived. For a moment, panic closed my throat.

I let my eyes do the searching first. At the very edge of the light, among the moldy boxes and snaking extension cords, I saw what looked like the handled ends of shovels. I plowed my way through the debris on the floor, hoping I didn't trip and find myself in a pile of rusted, rotting trash.

Three shovels leaned against a dusty, old fridge. I pulled and pulled until one loosened from the junk. I heard a crack as the long wooden shaft of the shovel came free, without the blade. I gently tugged on the next one, rocking the handle back and forth to get it out and avoid breaking it. It came loose, but just as the blade emerged from the gloom, it hooked itself on something, causing the rotted wooden shaft in my hand to snap and crumble. I sighed.

I lifted the final shovel out, closing my eyes and saying a little prayer. I felt the vibration of the blade as it scraped along the fridge. It emerged, fully intact, and other than a rusted tip, was in excellent condition.

I hoisted the shovel onto my shoulder, hitting the edge of the light above me with a clang. The light swayed, sweeping back and forth, illuminating the rear of the shed before plunging it into creepy shadows. I looked back one more time and thought I could see the curved end of a sled. I stood in the semidarkness, straining to see what else was hiding back there. I scanned the floor, trying to find a clear path. Getting to it was going to require me to go through an obstacle course of clutter, spiderwebs, and other things I couldn't see.

I hadn't been sledding since before we came here. We had the perfect hill on the far side of the river. I leaned the shovel against the side of the shed, swallowed my fear, and kept my eyes on the sled. It was worth the effort. The sled was in perfect condition, aside from the blooms of rust sprinkled on the metal runners. It glided easily over the snow as I hauled it behind me, making my way to Hannah's trailer.

"Spread the word," I told her. "We can all meet on the far side of the river after services."

"Where the hill is?"

"Yeah. We can slide down the hill and across the river."

Hannah's brows creased in the middle. "Do you think it's safe?"

I nodded. "It's been cold enough for days. I noticed yesterday that the top was frozen solid, and I couldn't see the water running under the surface. That means it's thick enough."

My brother had taught me that when we were exploring the ravine and frozen creek behind our house. I was scared to cross, afraid of falling through, so my brother went first. In the middle of the creek, he jumped up and down on the ice.

"See?" he shouted. "It'll hold. When you can't see the water below, it's fine."

When I got to the riverbank, Hannah was already on the other side with Noah and James. I stepped onto the slippery surface of the river and looked down. I couldn't see anything but ice. I took another tentative step, listening for the cracking, but nothing happened.

"C'mon, slowpoke," James shouted. "Get over here!"

"Where's Abby?" I asked, stepping onto the frozen bank.

"Chores," Noah answered with a shrug.

We climbed the hill, and I felt flutters in my stomach. From the top, it looked scarier than it did from the bottom. I was nervous and excited at the same time.

"Who wants to go first?" I asked.

"You should," Hannah said. "You found the sled."

"OK. Can someone hold the back while I sit on it?"

"I got it," Noah said, squatting down to grip the back end with both hands.

I climbed into the middle of the sled and sat down. I crossed my legs, then uncrossed them, sticking them out in front of me.

"Ready?" Noah asked.

"I'm ready."

"OK. One … two … three … whee!"

Noah let go and I was off, racing down the hill. I hit a small bump and was in the air for a split second, laughing the whole way. The sled was faster than I had anticipated and in what felt like five seconds, I was sliding across the snow and ice on the river. When I hit the riverbank on the opposite side, my friends whooped and cheered.

Over the next three hours, the crowd of kids grew. We all took turns flying down that hill and whooshing across the river. With only one sled, it was a test of patience and kindness, especially for the smaller kids. We went down solo, or in pairs, on our bottoms, or on our bellies. James built up the bump in the hill so we could really soar. Regardless of how old we were, we all laughed and screamed just the same.

Joseph was the youngest in our group. At six years old, he was missing his two front teeth.

"Dis is a great thled, Ruf," he lisped, turning around from the middle of the sled. "Fank you for finding it."

I grinned at him. "Are you ready? I'm letting go in one …
two … three!"

Joseph threw one arm in the air as he whizzed down the hill.
"Woohoooooooo!" we heard as he neared the bump. He hit it and
was in the air, higher than we had seen anyone go yet. We saw
Joseph's bottom lift off the sled, and he grabbed onto the edges
to secure himself. The sled landed smack in the middle of the
river, spinning around so Joseph was looking back at us, then
sliding about a foot before coming to a complete stop.

"AWETHOME!!!" Joseph yelled, throwing both arms in
the air.

And then he was gone.

It took all of us on that hill longer than it should have to
figure out that Joseph had gone through the ice.

James was the first to leap into action. He ran down that hill,
with Noah and Hannah right behind him. At the river's edge, he
stopped and shouted Joseph's name.

Then he shouted again. And again. He gingerly put one foot
on the ice, and I heard the crack even from the top of the hill
where I was frozen in fear.

James told Noah to go upstream to the left, Hannah downstream to the right. They were spreading out, not knowing if the
current had carried Joseph away or if he was stuck where he
went through.

Go help them, I said to myself. But my feet wouldn't move.
This is all my fault. It was my idea. I pushed him down that hill.

While my friends were trying to find Joseph, I stood alone.
The other kids had made their way down the hill and one of them
ran to the village to get help. Except for the rushing of the river
in the hole where Joseph used to be, there was silence.

I was rooted to my spot, like my boots had frozen to the
ground. The world around me got fuzzy at the edges. In my
mind, I replayed what had happened. *Did I hear the ice crack at*

all when I went down the first time? I was too busy having fun, enjoying the freedom of flying down the hill with speed I couldn't—and didn't want to—control. I was having a blast on a sunny winter day. I was lost in how I used to be, when I was Zoe. Ruth would never have allowed this to happen.

My thoughts were interrupted by a splash and the cracking of more ice. I snapped out of my reverie in time to see Abraham's body slip into the water. He took a deep breath, then dove under. After what felt like forever, he came back up, took another breath, and went under again.

My feet came to life, propelling me down the hill to join the others. When I stopped, standing with the little kids, my face was wet with tears.

Please don't be dead. Please don't be dead. Please. Please. Please.

Hannah, James, and Noah paced back and forth along the bank, scanning the ice for any sign of Joseph. Every few feet, James would test the ice at the bank, seeing if it was strong enough to hold him, but it cracked with even the slightest pressure.

Downstream, I could hear what sounded like someone snapping their fingers, but the noises were too close together for someone to be making that sound. The ice down river looked like it was breathing, rising up, then receding. I heard another loud crack before an arm erupted through the ice.

We all ran in that direction. James was the first on the ice, slipping as he made his way to the new hole. He lay down on his stomach, then reached out to grab hold of the arm that was pulling at the ice around the hole. Their hands grasped each other in an awkward handshake, before the arm from the river slipped back under.

I held my breath, and I think everyone else did too. Then the water burst from the hole and with it, a body. Joseph's limp form landed on his side on the ice with a sickening thud. My throat closed over the vomit threatening to come out.

James moved quicker than lightning. Standing up, he grabbed Joseph by the jacket, dragging him to the shore. I heard the jacket ripping as the water-logged material froze to the surface. James was half walking, half running, trying to get Joseph to shore without further cracking the ice and having them both fall through.

Abraham pulled himself out of the water, using his forearms to propel his body forward onto the ice. Once he was out, he rolled away from the hole and ran to where Joseph lay, inert and slightly gray.

Dropping to his knees, Abraham leaned over and placed his mouth over Joseph's blue lips, pinched his nose, and started to blow. Time stopped as I watched our leader try to breathe life into the boy.

Abraham pulled his mouth off Joseph's. He gently picked up the boy's wrist, checking for a pulse. He placed Joseph's arm at his side. Abraham said something to James, who ran off toward the village. He leaned over Joseph's chest and used both hands to apply repeated pressure. I watched him perform CPR, trying to pound him to life.

Please live. Please live. Please breathe.

Seven-year-old Lily came up to me and slipped her hand in mine, her bottom lip trembling. I knew she was trying to hold back her tears.

"He'll be OK, Lily," I said, looking down at her with what I hoped was a reassuring smile. "He's got to be OK."

Lily squeezed my hand in response but didn't say anything. My words were as much for me as they were for her.

Just when I thought I would pass out from fear, Joseph sputtered to life. Abraham turned the boy onto his side, and water choked out of his mouth. Joseph's eyes fluttered open and he tried to sit up. Abraham, his hand on the boy's shoulder, gently pushed him back down. Joseph coughed once then threw up.

When James came back with a thick wool blanket, Abraham turned to all of us on the other shore.

"Head back upstream," he said, pointing his chin in that direction. "The ice is thicker there and it will be safer to cross. Ruth, please make sure the children get home safely."

He held my gaze. I saw anger smoldering there. I knew he knew I was the one who brought the sled. James must have told him. I could make things right by taking care of the rest of the kids and getting them home safely. I would prove that I could be trusted, that this was just a freak accident.

As we walked back to the village, some of the kids were crying, while others stoically held back their tears. Noah, James, and Hannah said nothing to me or each other. A couple of kids stared vacantly ahead, in shock. I didn't know what to say to bring them back.

We were halfway to the village when I was greeted by parents running toward the river. Word had obviously spread. Moms and dads scooped up their children, wrapping them in tight hugs and tears.

Once all the children were either picked up by or delivered to their families, I parted from my friends without another word. I returned to our trailer, hoping my mom was there so I could get a hug of my own, but no one was home.

I lay down on my bed, wrapping my bedspread around me and over my head, feeling sorry for myself. I had wanted the comfort of my mother's arms, have her rub my back and tell me it was going to be OK, that it was just an honest mistake. I wanted my father to put his hands on my shoulders before hugging me tightly, grateful that nothing worse had happened and that I was safe. I imagined myself surrounded by their love.

The slamming of the trailer door snapped me out of my

exhausted sleep. I struggled to sit up, trapped in the wrapping of my blanket. When I peeled myself out, my father stood at the foot of my bed, fisted hands by his side. My mother stood beside him, arms crossed in front of her.

"Get out of bed, now," my father hissed.

I rose but sat at the edge, my legs shaking too much to support me.

"Do you have any idea what you've done?" he yelled. "What possessed you to do something so stupid?"

I wanted to have some fun, I thought. *I'm sorry*, I wanted to say, but the words wouldn't form themselves around my tongue.

"That boy could have died," he continued. "It's a miracle that he didn't, and we must pray he won't have any brain injury from almost drowning. You have no idea the damage you've done … what I've had to do to convince Abraham to not throw us out of here." Flecks of spit flew from his mouth, landing on my jeans and bed and face.

He leaned forward, getting close to my face and looking into my eyes. "You disappoint me."

I turned away from him toward my mother. I had hoped to see some compassion there, an ally. But she was tight-lipped, shaking her head.

My father stormed out of the trailer without letting me explain myself or make my apologies.

My mother didn't move.

"I didn't expect this kind of behavior from you, Ruth. I thought you would have known better. I thought you would take a minute to consider your actions and decisions before you almost caused a mother to lose her child. I suggest you sit here and think of a way to fix what you've done."

She shook her head again, then left me alone in the trailer.

I listened to the sound of her footsteps moving away. I didn't know what to do. Should I go see Joseph's parents and beg for forgiveness? Should I run away and make everyone's life easier?

I had to fix this. Every time I tried to be truly me, things went wrong. When I followed the rules and forgot about life before, things went great. When I worked to make my parents, Abraham, and everyone else happy, they showered me with praise and love.

I knew what I had to do. I had to bury the Zoe part of me forever.

zoe

fifteen

IT WAS STILL DARK when I woke. This was the worst part about the start of winter. The sun didn't rise until after seven o'clock in the morning and was settled below the horizon before we even had dinner. I pulled the covers over my head, drifting back to sleep, but a knock on my door woke me again, followed by a rough whisper of my name. I smiled. This morning, I was waking up as Zoe for the first time in years.

"Zoe, are you up?" It was Gary.

I turned my head to look at the clock radio sitting on the nightstand. The flickering red numbers on the ancient relic showed 6:46.

"I'm awake," I croaked, my voice not yet working properly. "Give me a second."

I swung my legs out of bed, allowing my sleepy brain a minute to recall what happened yesterday. There was no turning back now. I had made my choice when I announced my real name.

I grabbed my robe and shuffled to open the door. "Why are you waking me up so early?"

"I've got some news," Gary said, a big smile across his face. How he could look so happy and alive at this hour was beyond me.

"What's up?"

"Family services found your grandmother."

I stood there, blinking away sleep and disbelief. "How did

this happen so fast? My real grandmother? They know it's her for sure? Not some crazy person?"

Gary was already shaking his head. "It's her for sure. I called my supervisor after last night and she put the wheels into motion. The FBI and the police started the search and before midnight, they had found your grandmother. She's been granted what's called emergency guardianship. She didn't want to believe that you were alive. She's flying in from Montana this morning."

My heart beat wildly in my chest and my hands were instantly sweaty. I stood there, not sure what my next move should be.

"Isn't this exciting?" Gary asked. "I wanted to get you up early so you could shower and gather your things together. I brought you something."

I hadn't even noticed he had been holding his hands behind his back the whole time he stood in the doorway. He brought one arm forward and with it came a bright blue suitcase on wheels.

"Every kid comes in here with almost nothing, and what they do have is usually in a garbage bag or two. When you leave, I want to make sure you have something. This is yours now."

He held the suitcase out toward me. It was small and shiny, its surface smooth and obviously brand new. Gary pulled the handle out from the top and tilted it in my direction.

"Thanks," I said, reaching out and taking it. I twirled it around on its wheels. I remembered my last suitcase, where my former self had been burned into a pile of ashes.

"Come on down when you're ready. Maria is on her way to make you a special goodbye breakfast. Your grandmother will be here around ten o'clock this morning."

As soon as I wheeled the suitcase into the room and closed the door behind me, every part of my body came alive, like my blood was moving too fast through my veins. I sank down on my bed, clenching and unclenching my fists. I jiggled my legs, trying to still myself from the outside in.

I slid down to the floor, leaned against the bed, and tried to bring my grandmother's face into my mind. I remembered her dark brown hair tied into a thick braid down her back, but her face was a fuzzy memory. I can't even remember the last time I saw her, but it had to be before I turned eight. That was the first birthday party she didn't come to. It was the first family celebration we'd had since Eric died, and I figured she was too sad to come. And then we were gone, on our way to Idaho less than four months later.

Grandma Lottie.

Would I recognize her when she came? I looked out the window and saw the sky was starting to lighten up. My head filled with a million questions.

Would she be happy to see me?

What were her rules going to be?

What was her house like?

Would I have my own room?

Did she blame me for what happened to my parents?

I let these thoughts swirl in my head as I collected the donated clothing and folded them into the suitcase. The toilet in the bathroom flushed, making me realize I should probably get in there to shower before everyone else was up and I had to wait my turn. Packing wasn't going to take long, but I wanted time to stand under the warm water and do some more thinking. I was terrified of what my life would look like from now on.

When I was done, I wiped my hand across the bathroom mirror, slicing through the fog. I gazed at my reflection, running my shaky hands through my wet and stringy hair. A new worry wormed its way into my brain. Who was Lottie expecting me to be? She didn't know anything about what had happened to me over the past seven years. But I didn't know anything about her either. I was going to have to figure things out as I went along. That's what Mom told me we needed to do when we first moved into the trailer at the commune.

"When you don't know what the rules are, you need to watch and learn from those who do," she told me. "We will learn as we go."

I missed her and Dad so much. I closed my eyes and listened to the sound of their voices as they played in my head, hoping they would never fade.

"Yeah, so, Zoe, huh?" Maria showed up as promised and was already making waffles when I walked into the kitchen.

The rest of the kids were hanging around in the living room with Gary. The television was on, tuned to some sports channel.

"Please don't make a thing about this." I slid onto a kitchen chair and put my head in my hands.

"I wasn't gonna. Just checking to see if the name sticks."

"I've been Ruth for so long, it was the name I told them when they found me under that coop. Pretty stupid, I guess."

Maria's ponytail bounced from side to side as she shook her head. "What kid hasn't had an identity crisis?" She turned her back on the waffle iron and sat across from me. "When I was seventeen and trying to figure out my life without my parents, I snuck into clubs and told every guy I met my name was Harmony."

"Why?"

"Because I could be someone else. A girl who flirted and danced and got happy drunk—yes, I was underage—and not an orphan with a train wreck of a life."

"When did you decide to stick to Maria?"

"When my grief caught up with me. I realized I could change my name, but it would never change what had happened to me."

The waffle iron beeped. Maria stood to take off the freshly finished waffles and poured more batter for the next batch.

"Do you make waffles every time someone leaves here?"

She nodded. "I know I make a big deal about it and it's not even my life, but I remember what it feels like to be reunited with family."

"You know not everyone gets a happily ever after, right?" I pointed out.

"Why so glum, chum? Your grandma is coming to get you. Aren't you happy about that?"

I shrugged my shoulders. What if I didn't like her, or worse, what if she didn't want me? I was relieved when Maria turned back to the waffle iron and resumed cooking.

The plate she put in front of me when we all sat down in the dining room had two waffles, decorated with chocolate chips and rainbow sprinkles, topped with a tower of whipped cream. The waffles were perfect, crispy at the first bite, and then melted on my tongue.

"You know," I said around a mouthful, "if you want people to be excited about leaving here, you probably shouldn't make such a delicious breakfast for them. If I were you, I'd consider burning bacon and undercooking eggs."

Maria laughed, her smile stretching right into her eyes. I kind of wished I had time to get to know her better.

"Are you nervous?" Gary asked.

I kept my focus on my plate. I wanted to tell him I was scared, nervous, excited, worried, sad, and confused, but I kept all my words and feelings inside. My stomach felt like it was full of butterflies instead of waffles.

"It's normal to feel that way, you know," he said, reading my mind. "You've had a lot of stuff going on. It's OK to be a mixed bag of feelings."

We devoured breakfast, chatting about nothing. We avoided conversations about the upcoming Christmas season, a terrible subject for kids without families. I heard the crunch of tires on the snow-covered driveway. Gary was already out of his chair, heading to the front door. I glanced at Maria, who was dabbing at her eyes with a napkin. The butterflies in my stomach were squashed down by rocks.

"I don't do ugly goodbyes, but good luck … Zoe." I turned in my chair and looked at Gia. She had been sitting on the other side of the table, but at the far end and had avoided looking at me. "I think that name suits you better than Ruth. Go and be her." She nodded once and walked away, but not before I noticed the tears in her eyes.

"Turn on your light, Gia," I said to her back, echoing the advice she once gave me.

From where I was sitting at the table, I had a clipped view of the front door. It swung open, and I watched a pair of fur-trimmed winter boots step over the threshold. Two black leather gloves reached down to pull the boots off and I was surprised to see purple socks. Must be a visitor for someone else. It couldn't be my grandma. Who over the age of eighteen wore purple socks?

I strained to hear what Gary and this visitor were saying, but the noise at the table was too loud and I was too far from the foyer to hear anything clearly. I watched the socks move toward the dining room and slowly let my eyes travel up. I took in the skinny jeans, the long-sleeve shirt with the puffy vest layered on top, and the knit cap covering her head. My eyes rested on the necklace: two circles intertwined, one of silver bamboo and one of small black stones. I felt the surrounding room vanish as my eyes traveled up and landed on my father's blue-gray eyes on someone else's face.

"Zoe," I heard Gary say, "your grandmother is here."

The table fell silent in an instant. Time froze as my grandmother and I stared at each other. And then the room erupted with noise as the other kids began clearing the table and taking everything into the kitchen. All I could do was scrape my memory banks for my history with this woman. Random images flickered through my mind. A game show on television. Dry and tasteless pork chops. Tea cups with flowers I wasn't allowed to use.

"Hi, Zoe," she said, crossing her hands in front of her stomach. "Do you … do you remember me?"

I dropped my gaze to her lips for a second, wanting her to repeat my name so I could see how it came out of her mouth. When I looked back up, I saw a flicker of hope in her eyes. I'd last seen that look in my dad's eyes when he told us we were moving and tried to sell it as a great adventure.

I shook my head. How was it that my grandmother was a stranger to me?

"I guess I shouldn't be surprised," my grandmother said. "It's been a long time, Zoe. Let me reintroduce myself. My name is Lottie. Your father was my son."

She took a step forward and instinctively my body recoiled. If she thought I was going to hug her, she had another thing coming. I do not hug strangers.

"I just want to shake your hand," she said, a small smile playing across her lips. "I don't like to hug people I barely know."

She extended her hand to me, and I took it. Her palm was soft, but she gripped my hand firmly, then put her other hand on top.

"It's nice to see you again," she said. When she smiled, the corners of her eyes crinkled, and my father's face flashed before me. The sadness punched me in the stomach and a small puff of air pushed out of my mouth. Nobody seemed to notice, though.

"So … can we just go?" Lottie asked Gary.

"Legally, there is nothing stopping you."

Lottie turned to me. "Are *you* ready to go?" she asked.

"Umm … I … uh," I stuttered, unsure how to answer. Too many things were happening too fast.

"Let's go make sure you've got all your things, Zoe," Gary suggested.

I followed him up the stairs to my room, my legs heavy with every step. I had just started to feel comfortable and now I had to leave. I should have told Lottie no. I'm not ready.

"Do you need a few more days here?" Gary asked. "I can set it up so you and Lottie can get acquainted slowly."

"Yes, but also no," I answered. "It's best to rip off the Band-Aid, right?"

Gary smiled and nodded. He picked up my suitcase, and I followed him back down the stairs. Lottie and Maria stood in the dining room, but their conversation stopped when I approached.

"I'm ready," I said to the floor.

Lottie took a short breath in through her nose. "We've got plenty of daylight left. Let's hit the road," she announced.

"You're driving back to Montana?" Gary asked.

Lottie nodded. "I rented a car. I thought it would be a good way for Zoe and me to get reacquainted. Six hours in a car should give us enough time."

"That's a great idea," Gary said.

No, it's not.

"Wait," I blurted out. "I thought you flew here."

"I did. It's been a long time since I've had a road trip, and I thought you might enjoy it too. It's only a day of driving. We can see some sights, eat junk food, drink soda, and take our sweet time."

"That sounds fun." Gary's positivity prickled like cactus needles.

"I get carsick," I announced.

"You do?" Gary asked. "You did OK when we drove here from the hospital."

"Short trip," I mumbled. "It would be faster to fly," I pointed out.

"Are you in a hurry to go somewhere?" Lottie asked.

I looked down at the floor and shook my head.

"Good. Me neither."

There were best wishes from Maria and handshakes from Gary. Before I could put up a fight, I was in the front seat of a MINI Cooper convertible.

"Couldn't you get a bigger car with a real roof?" I questioned, not trying to keep the sarcasm out of my voice.

My grandmother settled into her seat, pulled the belt across her shoulder, and started the car without saying a word. As we pulled away from the house, I looked back over my shoulder to wave to Gary and Maria, but the front door was closed and nobody was there.

sixteen

MY GRANDMOTHER REMAINED silent as we drove away. I knew we were heading north to Montana. We studied geography at school in the commune, but I had already memorized all the states in first grade.

I gasped, sitting forward in my seat as a clear memory came to me.

"Are you OK?" Lottie asked, glancing over at me.

"I … I think I just remembered something." I turned my head to look at her profile. There was my dad's nose that sloped at the tip like a mini ski jump.

"You bribed me," I said. "You told me if I memorized the fifty states, you'd buy me Chrissa Maxwell."

"I'm not following you. What are you talking about?"

I paused, trying to recall what my grandmother said to me all those years ago.

"She was an American Girl doll. When I was six, you gave me two months to memorize the names of all the states and bought me Chrissa when I did."

"Oh my god! I remember that." Her face wrinkled as she smiled. "Remember the bonus content?"

"Washington, D.C., is not a state," I recited, "but was established as the District of Columbia to be the seat of the government of the United States. That earned me Chrissa's craft table with the tiny sewing machine."

"And what else?"

I glanced out my window, the morning sun warming my face. I remembered the bright rectangular red box with Chrissa's face peering out from the plastic. The craft table came in a square red box. I closed my eyes and called to mind a smaller red box my grandmother gave me.

"Oh! Starburst! Chrissa's llama! You got her for me when I labeled all the states on a map."

"That's right." She nodded. "I tricked you into learning how to spell too. Whatever happened to that doll?"

My smiled faded. Mom didn't let me pack Chrissa when we were leaving. My beloved doll and her accessories went into a garbage bag we donated to a thrift shop.

"I'm not sure," I lied. "With the move … we left so fast …" I didn't finish the sentence, letting Lottie fill in the blank.

She pressed her lips together and gave her head a slight nod. "I will buy you a new doll, if you like."

I blinked back my tears. It was a kind offer, and I knew my grandmother was extending an olive branch. I was too old for dolls, anyway, and a new American Girl would only remind me of everything I had lost.

"Thanks, but I'm past dolls now."

Through the windshield, I watched the city of Idaho Falls thin out, the view changing from houses to boxy warehouses.

"I need to ask you something," she said, letting the topic of the doll drift away. "I read in the newspaper that your name was changed to Ruth. Do you want me to call you that?"

I shook my head.

"OK. Good. Zoe, it is."

Eventually, the warehouses outside the window dwindled and for the next two hours, the view on either side of the highway was rocks and trees and flat landscape. That's all. The stillness in the car was cut by the music and chatter coming from the radio. I wondered if my grandmother was waiting for me to start the conversation. Since the chaos at the commune, everyone tiptoed around me, being careful about what they said and how they said it. I heard words whispered when they thought I couldn't hear, words like *trauma, therapy, adjustment,* and *normal.*

What did normal even mean?

If anyone had asked me how I was feeling as we rolled quietly down the highway, I wouldn't have been able to give them an answer. There was no one emotion to land on. I switched between numbness and feeling like my heart was imploding one vessel at a time. I missed my parents and my friends and felt their absence every minute of the day. I felt like I had taken off a cozy sweater in an icy room. Did I suffer any mental damage? Of course I did. Am I damaged? Probably. Will I ever be "normal"? Not likely.

And now I was sitting in the front seat of a tiny car with a woman I barely knew, driving to a place I could hardly remember.

"We're going to stop and fill up with gas," Lottie said, puncturing the quiet when a service area came into view. She pulled off the highway and stopped in front of a pump. There were two small brick buildings behind the pumps, both trimmed in wood that looked new, with a rich, reddish-brown color. One building's sign read A Plus Convenience; the other read AA Plus Pizza.

"Here," Lottie said, holding out twenty dollars. "Go into the store and get us some snacks. Coke, water, and a big bag of caramel M&M's for me. You can get whatever you want for yourself."

I looked at the bill and then at the woman beside me. Both were foreign.

"I ... I don't know what I'm supposed to do."

"You take the money, go inside, pick out some things, and pay. Simple."

Lottie waved the bill, and when I still didn't take it dropped it in my lap. She got out of the car, turning her attention to the gas pump.

"Jumping in is the best way to move forward," she said to the gas tank, but I knew she was talking to me.

I picked up the bill and went inside. The man behind the counter looked up and said hello.

"What can I help you find today, miss?" He smiled. He was wearing a black-and-red-checked shirt, perfect attire for being in the middle of Nowhere, Idaho, at the end of November.

"I'm good, thanks," I muttered, scanning the layout of the store. His eyes did the same on my face. The space between his eyebrows crinkled, then he cocked the right one, and his mouth opened into an *O* like he'd just figured something out.

"I'm happy to help. It's not every day that we get someone famous in here."

I stared at him, not understanding what he was saying.

"You're that kid from the commune. The one who lived."

Heat burned my ears and flooded my cheeks. All those photographers must have printed photos of me somewhere. I fled to the back of the store, looking for a place to hide and calm down. I opened the tall cooler, letting the cold air wash over me. I hadn't expected to be recognized. I pulled out a bottle of water and held it to the back of my neck to calm the fire.

For seven years, I'd blended into the background. As Ruth, life was simple. It took me a long time to stop trying to be Zoe and now that I was free to be me, I almost wanted to be Ruth again. Invisible. Unremarkable. Just like everyone else.

My stomach clenched before the lights in the store got brighter and the smells of burnt coffee and floor cleaner filled my nostrils. As I stared at all the stuff I didn't recognize, I felt my fury trying to push itself out of my body. I wanted to scream. I wanted to violently push everything off the shelves. I had been manipulated for years into becoming Ruth. How long would it take me to find my way back into this foreign world as Zoe?

My vision swirled and I was sweating all over. Using the bottom of my sweatshirt, I wiped my forehead, but there was nothing I could do about the wetness in my armpits. I took a deep breath, reining in my anger. I walked the aisles, over-whelmed with the choices.

At the commune, money never changed hands. We got the food we needed from the garden and from the shed that func-tioned as the pantry for everyone. There was never a lot to choose from, but sometimes Mom let me pick out linguini, my favorite kind of pasta. Now, I stared at the shelves stocked with crackers, soup, bread, canned chili, and medicine. Everything I picked up slipped from my sweat-slicked hands.

I made my way back to the bank of coolers and opened one of the doors. I let the cool air wash over me again as I examined the eggs, milk, yogurt, and an assortment of sandwiches already made and wrapped in plastic. I wiped my hands on my jeans before grabbing a couple of bottles of Coke, another bottle of water, and two bags of caramel M&M's.

When I approached the cash register, the man was leaning over the counter, arms crossed over each other.

"So, you heading to Yellowstone?" he asked, taking my items.

I shook my head and shrugged my shoulders at the same time. "I don't think so."

"Shame, since it's so close," he pointed out. "It's a good time to go. It'll be quiet and you'll probably be able to see some bison."

I shrugged again and passed him the $20 bill.

"Good luck," he shouted after me as I rushed out the door.

I froze as soon as I was outside. There wasn't a single car at the pumps. I raced around the side of the building, but there was nothing but an empty bench and a garbage can. I followed the brick wall to the back and only found dumpsters there. My heart hammering in my chest, I returned to the front of the store, praying my grandmother was there. A single car pulled up, a large SUV, and I irrationally hoped maybe Lottie had simply changed cars. When a middle-aged man climbed out, my throat closed. I choked back tears, pacing in front of the store, bag swinging by my side. Lottie had left me.

With every second that passed, my thoughts became more frenzied. *What do I do? Where do I go? Why did she do this? Why can't anyone love me enough to stay?*

"You shouldn't swing the bag like that," I heard my grand-mother say. "You're shaking the soda and now I won't be able to open it."

I stopped pacing and let relief flood over me. Lottie was standing in front of the building next door, holding a pizza box.

I forced myself to breathe normally as I got into the car parked around the side of the pizza place and placed the bag on the floor between my legs.

"Lucky for me I saw that, or I'd be wearing Coke the second I opened it," she said, pushing her seat forward to put the pizza in the back.

The way she was speaking made me wonder if she was mad. She was smiling, but her lips were pressed together. She started the car and pulled away.

"Just give me the water." She sighed, holding her hand out for the bottle.

She grabbed it from me and used her teeth to twist off the cap. She never took her eyes off the road, not even when she tilted the bottle too soon and water dribbled down the front of her shirt.

"Looks like I was destined to get my shirt wet."

I didn't know whether to laugh. If this had been my dad, he would have been laughing his head off.

The smell of the pizza filled the tiny car. Lottie reached back, and my mouth watered instantly when she opened the box and ripped two slices from the pie.

"I hope you like pepperoni. Do you want some?" she asked.

"Yes, please." I took a slice and chomped off the triangle end.

"Oh my, this is delicious," my grandmother mumbled around a mouthful of semi-hot pizza. "This pepperoni is perfectly crispy."

"I haven't had pizza for a long time," we both said at the same time.

Lottie and I whipped our heads to look at each other. She was smiling widely; I was stunned that we had something in common.

"When was the last time you had pizza?" I asked.

She looked up to the roof of the car, and I could tell she was trying to remember.

"I think it was probably almost ten years ago. It was at your …" Lottie stopped talking. When I glanced over, her eyes were filled with tears.

"At my house?" I asked. "The day of Eric's first chemo treatment at the hospital?"

I had come home after school that day to find Lottie sitting in the living room. I was six years old, and I didn't know how sick Eric was. I was annoyed that my parents thought I needed a babysitter, but my grandmother fed me snacks and put a movie into the DVD player. We sat on the couch with a plate of cookies and a bowl of popcorn between us. When my parents came home, emotionally drained from the day, Mom ordered pizza while Dad carried Eric up the stairs and put him to bed.

My own eyes filled with tears at the memory. I had been

clueless about what was really going on with Eric. At the time, I thought it was funny that my dad had to carry my twelve-year-old brother up the stairs like a baby. Six months of chemotherapy treatment would pass before my parents sat me down to tell me Eric wasn't going to be OK.

"That was the last time I had pizza too," I whispered.

We drove in silence for a while, Lottie chewing on her food, me lost in my memories. The pizza in my hand had gone cold, but I took a bite, anyway.

"You know, I was so excited when your parents named you Zoe. Did you know in Greek it means 'life'?"

I shook my head. "No one ever told me that."

"I'm sorry," Lottie murmured. "I'm sorry for everything you've gone through. I'm sorry that I just vanished from your life when you needed me the most. You know there was nothing I could do, right? Your father didn't tell me you were moving. You were all there one day and gone the next."

I swallowed the half-chewed bite lodged in my throat.

"I miss them." That was all I could say before the sobs erupted from me. I curled my body away from my grandmother and brought my knees to my chest. I howled and grunted, trying to release all the pain and sorrow. I had been holding everything in for so long, but now the dam burst. Even though I barely knew her, Lottie made me feel safe and that made all my grief gush out.

My sleeves were soaking wet from wiping my tears. When my tears stopped, I felt lighter inside, like I had been holding a hundred-pound weight inside my chest and it finally lifted. I don't know how long I was crying, but I looked up just as we passed a Welcome to Montana sign. I stared out the window, watching the trees go by. I gradually became aware of the fact that my grandmother had said nothing the whole time I was sobbing. She drove in silence, letting me cry myself empty.

When the trees on my side of the car thinned out and I was staring across the snowy open plain, my grandmother finally decided to speak.

"I miss them too. The way your father snatched you away from me was just as sudden as your loss."

"My parents were murdered," I hissed. "Every family who welcomed me into their home is dead. All my friends burned to a crisp. How is that even remotely the same?"

Lottie took a breath through her nose and blew it out her mouth. "It's not … I'm just … I meant … shit. It sucks for both of us. I was trying to say I know how it feels to be left behind."

I turned my body toward the window again, crossing my arms over my chest. This car was too small for so much pain. There was no way to escape the gloom coming from both of us. Lottie must have felt it too because she rolled her window down halfway, letting the icy November air in.

She sighed as we passed a sign that read WEST YELLOW-STONE MONTANA. DESTINATION, ADVENTURE.

"Listen," Lottie said, "I want you to know that I'll be here for you when you are ready to talk about what happened. I'd like to know what life was like in the commune. I want to hear about your friends and school, or anything, even the bad stuff."

Still, I remained silent, my eyes taking in the change of scenery from open fields to mountains. *Zoe Kane,* I thought. *Destination, Unknown.*

seventeen

ONCE WE WERE CLOSED in by mountains on both sides of the road, Lottie had to turn off the radio because there was nothing but static. The only noise in the car was the humming of the tires on the asphalt.

The peaks reminded me of the mountains surrounding the commune. We had been so far away from them then, and now I was passing through, close enough to touch them. Nothing was familiar to me. I'd been gone seven years, and I was now completely lost in my own home state. Nothing along the route triggered memories.

We twisted the caps off our Cokes and tore open our packets of M&M's.

"Get ready for a life-changing experience." Lottie smiled. She popped a candy into her mouth, and I did the same. She laughed when she saw how wide my eyes went when I bit through the candy shell and sank my teeth into the caramel and chocolate. I had never tasted anything so buttery and salty-sweet at the same time. She laughed again when I let out a burp after the first few gulps of soda.

"It's so sweet," I said, "but somehow refreshing at the same time." I thought of the Coke I'd had with Gia. I said a silent prayer that she would soon find her place in the world.

"Just wait until the heat of summer. An ice-cold Coke is the best thing when it feels like the sun is trying to fry you."

Every town we drove through matched perfectly to the

descriptions of main streets I had read about in books: a stop sign, one or two traffic lights, a post office, a coffee shop, a burger joint, a grocery store, a law office, a doctor's office, a pharmacy, and the tallest building only three stories high. All the parking spots were angled toward the storefronts, and everywhere I looked, people were shaking hands or hugging or engaged in what looked like lively conversations. Small-town America reminded me of the commune, where everyone knew each other and was genuinely happy to see their neighbors.

When we passed the sign for the Yellowstone River, I had a memory flash. I saw myself in the kitchen in our house on Black Diamond Road. My mother was sitting at the table, tightening the screws on the handles of the pots and pans, then in a flash, she was signing the form for a kindergarten field trip to Riverfront Park. I could smell the dish soap my father was using as he stood at the sink cleaning up after breakfast. I heard my brother's voice as he sat beside me, telling me about his own field trip to collect autumn leaves.

"I remember your house!" I exclaimed as another memory came, this one of the tire swing in her backyard. "It's on the other side of the freeway on Dogwood Drive, right?"

"I'm still there." She nodded. "Billings hasn't changed much. What else do you remember?"

I looked out the windshield and as we passed car dealerships, restaurants, gas stations, and strip malls, my mind filled with the faces of my old friends from school and gymnastics.

"I used to be really good at gymnastics. I went to Tumblebeans twice a week. And I went swimming sometimes on Saturdays at the Y. For lessons and free swim. I went to Sandhill Elementary School!" I was sitting forward now, the seat belt over my shoulder trying to pull me back.

"They tore that school down the year after you left," Lottie told me. "The roof started leaking after the spring rains and they found asbestos in the insulation and in the walls. The paint was full of lead. The whole building was too toxic to even try fixing."

A wave of sadness washed over me. Another piece of my life gone forever.

We turned onto a quiet street with small houses, all single level. The trees were naked, the lawns hidden under a white blanket of snow. The center of the road was clear where the cars drove, and the sun hit the ruts, melting the blackened mess. The snow that was left hugged the curbs of the street.

As my grandmother slowed down, I pressed my nose against the window, leaving a smudge. I pulled my face away when I saw a faded yellow stucco house with a deck in front.

"That's it! That's your house!" I screamed. "I used to sit on the railing of that deck and watch the cars go by. Mom always yelled at me to be careful and not fall off and smash my head open." Again, a bubble of pain bloomed in my chest.

Lottie slowed the car to a stop, then turned off the engine.

"Are you ready for this?" she asked, pulling off the cap she had worn the entire trip. Her short hair was still dark brown, like my dad's and my own, but with silver strands growing from the temples.

I shrugged.

She walked around the back of the car, pulling my suitcase from the trunk.

"What should I do with this pizza?" I called to her back.

"Bring it in," she said over her shoulder. Lottie was already at the front door, my suitcase beside her. I could hear the jingle of her keys as she unlocked the house.

I carried the pizza box with both hands, the smell of cold cheese wafting up and making me hungry again. As we walked into the kitchen, I willed my brain to remember, to bring back memories of laughter, meals, and family, but nothing came. I dropped the pizza onto the bright yellow table that sat against the far wall, across from the sink. Lottie stopped walking and turned around, pointing to the pizza box.

"Unless you plan to eat more now, that should go into the fridge."

I grabbed the box off the table and opened the fridge door. Inside, there was a bottle of wine, a salami log, and a loaf of bread. As I placed the pizza on an empty shelf, I noticed ketchup, mustard, mayo, and some sliced cheese in the door.

"Not much in here." I laughed.

"No sense in filling the fridge with food." She shrugged. "I didn't know how long I'd be gone."

I followed her down the narrow hallway to the back of the house, wheeling my suitcase behind me. Just outside the kitchen, I noticed stairs going down off to the side. On the left side of the hallway was the only bathroom, on the right was a good-size bedroom, and at the end of the hall was a second, smaller bedroom.

"This one will be yours," she said with a swoop of her arm.

Against one of the beige walls sat a double bed with a small nightstand beside it. On the opposite wall was a dresser. The only window in the room looked out onto the backyard. Cobwebs had collected in the corners near the ceiling, and dust coated everything. I let my suitcase plop on the floor, the dust cloud confirming the room had not been used in a very long time.

"Sorry." I winced, glancing at Lottie.

She leaned against the doorframe, watching me take in the room.

"This closet right here"—she pointed to a narrow door outside my bedroom—"is a pantry, but all the cleaning stuff is in here too. You probably want to wash the sheets and the blankets. Laundry is in the basement. This home is now your home, so you might as well get used to finding your way around. The living room and dining room are right over here." She pointed from halfway down the hall.

I walked over and poked my head through another doorway. There was a dining room table covered with a bright white tablecloth, and the living room was spotless. A gray couch sat across the room from a very big television. My eyes wandered from the TV to a fireplace that looked like it had never been used, then to two oversized armchairs sitting under the picture window at the front of the house. I stepped into the living room, walking toward the chairs, and saw the doorway circled back to the kitchen and the house's front door. It was small but cozy.

"I'm sure you want to get settled into your room, but obviously I need to go grocery shopping. Let's snack on some cold pizza while you tell me what you like to eat. Don't get your hopes up. I'm not much of a cook."

Lottie and I nibbled our pizza while I told her what I liked to eat for breakfast, lunch, and dinner. She asked about snacks and what kind of fruits and vegetables I didn't like. She didn't flinch when I asked for hummus (for dipping carrots and cucumber), hot sauce (for zesting up my eggs), and tuna (for sandwich melts). She wrote everything down in a small, coil-bound notebook she'd pulled out of her purse.

"Do you want to come with me?" she asked.

I shook my head. I wasn't ready for any more public appearances yet.

"If it's OK with you, I'd like to start some laundry and put my things away. Mop the floor, maybe."

"You're not here to clean," Lottie said as she pushed her chair away and stood up. "You can do whatever you want today."

"I don't mind. I like to keep busy." I shrugged. I was about to say that it was how I was raised, but the way Lottie pursed her lips and looked me over like she wanted to ask me something made me hold back.

"Suit yourself. I'll be gone for about an hour or two." She picked up her purse and was heading for the front door. She paused and turned back to me.

"Are you sure you'll be OK on your own?"

I nodded again.

Once she left the house, I went to my new bedroom, surveying the space. It was only slightly larger than the room I had at Gary's halfway house and at least twice the size of what I had in the trailer. It wasn't a great room, but it had potential. I could see where I might hang posters or pictures.

I unpacked, hanging some shirts on the wire hangers in the closet, and put the rest of my things in the top drawer of the three-drawer dresser. I pulled the sheets and quilt off the bed, then carried them to the laundry room at the bottom of the basement stairs. Once the washing machine was running, I took up the mop and pail I found tucked in a corner.

While I washed the hardwood floors, I became aware of the sparseness of the walls, the fireplace mantel, and the hutch in the dining room. There were a few knickknacks here and there, but there wasn't a single photograph anywhere. I gazed at the empty wall above the fireplace, noticing the lighter paint outline where a picture used to be. I distinctly remembered a family photo of all of us—my parents, me and Eric, Grandma Lottie and Grandpa Jake—hanging there. There was nothing there now, other than empty space and more cobwebs in the corners.

I cleaned for almost two hours, letting the monotony and repetition lull me into calm. When I made my bed, the smell of detergent gave me a deep sense of accomplishment. *Chores done well are always rewarded intrinsically*, Mom was fond of saying.

"Yoo-hoo!" Lottie called from the front door. "Zoe? Can you help me with the groceries?"

I pulled on the hoodie I had just taken out of the dryer and met her at the back of her gargantuan white SUV.

"This is a bit roomier than that MINI," I joked, counting twelve bags of groceries. "This holds way more than a suitcase and a box of pizza. Is this yours or another rental?"

"It's mine. I parked it at the airport when I came to get you." She picked up a bag and passed it to me. "I don't know how anyone can manage with a tiny car," she laughed.

Once the groceries were put away, Lottie joined me on the couch, where I sank back into the cushions. I turned my attention to the television, blankly staring at the images flashing across the screen. When a commercial came on showing a family laughing around a dinner table, my chest squeezed, like I was collapsing from the inside. I ran to the bathroom, where every bit of pizza I ate came back up.

eighteen

AFTER BRUSHING MY TEETH, I swished the water around in my mouth, working to get the bits of pizza out. I stared at myself in the mirror. Under each eye, dark circles masked freshly burst blood vessels. I hadn't thrown up so hard since I was twelve and Hannah and I both got algae poisoning from the contaminated water in the commune's swimming hole. Once we were done being sick, the punishment for sneaking away continued with scrubbing the mildew from every stall in the shower house.

I cupped my hands under the tap, then rinsed my face with ice-cold water. The shock felt good, distracting me from the pain of the memory of Hannah. *I hope it was quick and painless for you, Hannah.* After drying my face, I wandered back into the living room to say good night to Lottie.

"I'm really tired," I said when she commented about the early hour.

"Oh, by the way," she called out, "I stopped on my way home and signed you up for school. They've got you registered as a sophomore, but you have to take a test before you start."

"What? Why? When?"

"Which one should I answer first?" Lottie chuckled.

"I … I … don't think I'm ready for that," I sputtered.

"Since you've been out of school for seven years, you need to be tested so they know what you know."

"I haven't been out of school," I argued. "We had school in the commune. It was just different." I looked at the hand-me-down T-shirt I was wearing, fingering its worn hem. What did kids my age even wear to high school? My stomach flipped over at the thought.

"But you haven't been in a normal school. I can't give them a report card, Zoe. The only information they have is how you were doing when you left Sandhill Elementary. And that wasn't even a complete year. Your parents pulled you out in the middle of third grade."

I kept my eyes on my shirt and played with a loose thread. I wanted to hold on to the memory that flooded my mind: me and Mom on our annual back-to-school mall trip in the middle of August. It was always just me and her, since Eric never cared about what he wore on the first day and never wanted new binders or pencil cases or lunch coolers, like I did. Mom and I spent the whole day at the mall, enjoying the air-conditioning, eating in the food court, and picking out clothes. I was motivated to pick out a wardrobe quickly; if there was time before the mall closed, we would get our nails done.

"Why can't I do this test in the new year?"

"The sooner we know where you're at, the better. Besides," she said, pushing herself off the couch, "the principal and guidance counselor both felt starting at the beginning of the new semester would be less ... disorienting. It might take some time to get used to being in a structured classroom, but they said the first week of the new term is a good time to ease into things."

"I'm not ready," I protested. "What if everyone knows who I am and what happened to me? They'll think I'm either weird from living in a commune or messed up from being the only survivor."

"Or maybe they'll be kind and welcome you with open arms. It has to happen, Zoe. You have to go back to school. You have to start living again. It'll be good to have a normal high school life where kids vape in the bathroom and swear in the hallways and eat junk food their parents won't let them eat at home."

I really didn't want to go. I wanted to stay in Lottie's house where no one could see me. But a spark of excited curiosity ignited inside me. *The hard things are often the right things*, Abraham had said whenever someone put up a fight. I hated that his voice came into my head. I hated that he was right even more.

"When is the test?" I sighed.

"Monday. After school lets out."

"In four days? Don't I have to, like, study?"

"There is nothing you can do to prepare for this. The guidance counselor said the test has four sections—reading comprehension, math, science, and social studies multiple-choice questions."

"What happens if I fail? Will they make me go into ninth grade or …" I stopped, swallowing down the new round of puke that found its way into my throat. "What if they say I have to go back to middle school?" I squeaked. "I can't be in a class with twelve-year-olds!"

Lottie laughed. This was not funny at all. This was serious business.

"You won't be sent back to elementary, Zoe. You will go into tenth grade with all the other fifteen-year-olds, but the school wants to know where you might need help. They can arrange to have you in after-school tutoring or in-class extra help."

"No!" I screeched. "I can't have someone helping me in front of everyone! That would be so embarrassing."

Lottie reached over and pulled my hand from the unraveled thread.

"Honey," she said, "I'm sorry to say it, but you've been living like a wild child for the last seven years. I don't know specifically what happened every day at the commune, but I have to assume there are some holes, academically, socially, and developmentally." She squeezed my hand. I didn't—couldn't—do anything other than let my hand sit there like a cold, dead fish.

I knew from the look on her face that she had already made up her mind. There was no use protesting or trying to defend myself.

Again, I heard Abraham's voice in my head. *When people decide who you are, you cannot change their mind with words. It's the things you do that make them think different.*

I thought about telling my grandmother that life as a kid in a commune wasn't that different from the life I had before. I went to school every day. My parents made sure I finished my homework. I had chores that needed to be done before I was allowed to play with my friends. I had a bedtime and books to read and dishes to wash. Because of what Abraham had done, and how the media played the story, everyone on the outside had already decided the commune was a place full of crazies.

If I was going to change my grandmother's mind about me, I would have to ace that test, like Ruth would.

"Are you really nervous about the test?"

"A little."

"You'll do fine," she said. "You have Kane blood in your veins. We always land on our feet."

I didn't have the heart to tell her I had no idea who I was. But I appreciated her efforts to stitch us together as a family. I said good night as I softly closed the door to my bedroom.

I stood at my window, gazing at my reflection, and pressed my forehead to the glass. In the light spilling from my room, I could see the outline of the old ash tree in the backyard. The tire swing was now gone.

nineteen

I **WAS** a nervous wreck when I walked into the school Monday afternoon, even with Lottie at my side. I was dreading seeing anyone I might have once known, or worse, anyone who might know me from the newspapers or television. I was ready to learn, but I hadn't considered what it would be like to be back in a school with hundreds of kids. As we passed by the walls filled with framed photos of graduating classes from the last thirty years, I realized I wasn't ready to socialize again. I didn't know how to make friends anymore.

At the commune, we were all forced together and had to get along. There wasn't any hierarchy among us kids. We all had to shovel poop and hang laundry on the line and get our hands dirty pulling onions from the community garden. We gossiped among ourselves, had crushes on the cute boys, and rolled our eyes when our parents weren't looking.

My first day at school as Ruth had been a non-event. Miss Rebecca, who taught all the eight- and nine-year-olds, brought another desk into the classroom in the school trailer, handed me a notebook, some sharp pencils, and an eraser, and started the math lesson as if I had been there from the very start. Noah slid his desk closer to mine to share his textbook with me. I doubted it would be so easy to slide into life at Centennial High.

I was relieved when we made our way to the office without seeing another soul, other than the custodian mopping the stairs to the second floor.

I followed my grandmother into the main office. There were two people engaged in conversation, standing behind the long counter separating the students from the staff. When we walked in, they both looked up and smiled. The man moved to the counter, extending his hand toward me.

"You must be Zoe," he said as I weakly shook his hand. "Welcome to Centennial."

"Thanks," I uttered, making eye contact before quickly looking away.

"I'm Mr. Patterson, the guidance counselor here," he said, letting go of me, "and this is Mrs. Belkin. She's the administrator here. I'll be giving you the test, and we'll both hang around until you are done. Let's head over to my office. The sooner you get this started, the sooner you'll be free to enjoy the rest of your day."

We followed them down the central hall of the school and turned to the left. Halfway down that hall, we came to a door with Mr. Patterson's name on it. Inside, I was surprised to see a round table with comfortable-looking high-backed chairs, a love seat, a side table with a lamp, and a desk cleared of everything but a plant sitting in a corner. It looked more like a living room than an office in a high school.

"Have a seat at the table," Mr. Patterson said.

"Where should I wait?" Lottie asked.

"If it'll make Zoe more comfortable, you're free to wait in here, or …"

"I'll wait in the car," she interrupted. "Just come on out when you're done, Zoe."

Without another word or gesture, Lottie marched out of the office and left me.

"OK," Mrs. Belkin said, clapping her hands together. "Do you need any supplies? Pencils? Erasers? Sharpeners?"

I nodded.

"Which ones?"

"All of them," I answered. "I … I didn't know I had to bring anything. I'm sorry." I looked down at my shoes, trying to hide my embarrassment.

"We have whatever you need," Mr. Patterson said as he walked to his desk. He opened a drawer, pulling out two pencils, an eraser, and a pencil sharpener.

At the same time as he put the stuff on the table, Mrs. Belkin placed stapled papers in front of me. The title at the top read Aptitude Test.

"You can write your answers directly on these pages," Mrs. Belkin said. "There is no time limit here. When you are done, come back to the office with the test. Is there anything else you need?"

I shook my head.

"Excellent." Mr. Patterson smiled. "Good luck."

They walked out, but left the door open. I listened to their footsteps fade down the hallway. From my seat at the table, I looked around the room. On one wall hung a series of framed quotes meant to inspire me to be myself, follow my dreams, and find motivation. I stared at the bold lettering, wondering how words on glossy paper could really improve my situation. A thick layer of dust had settled on the top of the frames, and I wondered why no one had found the motivation to clean them.

I picked up the test papers and leafed through them. The test was divided into four parts, one for each of the core subjects. I started with math, since that was usually my best subject, working on three pages of problems. The algebra and trigonometry were complicated, and I left some of those questions with blanks in the answer spaces. Science and social studies required me to answer fifty multiple-choice questions for each. Some I knew the answers to while others were wild guesses.

I saved language arts for last. When I looked at the clock on the wall above the doorway, I saw that forty-five minutes had passed. Was that too soon to be almost finished? Miss Rebecca always encouraged us to take our time. *It's not a race to the finish line*, she would say. I failed the first test I had at the commune school. I was an angry eight-year-old who deliberately misspelled six out of the ten vocabulary words I had been given. At the time, I thought if I failed, we would be thrown out, and we could move back to Montana. Instead, Miss Rebecca gave me six lined sheets of paper and made me rewrite every misspelled word until both sides of every page were filled, one word per page. *Disappear, circumstance, believe, rhythm, pajamas,* and *niece,* scrawled sixty-six times.

For the language arts portion of the test, I had to read an essay about a girl and her dream to visit the place where her mother was born, then answer questions about content and symbolism.

Without warning, my chest tightened. I fought the tears threatening to flow and tried to take deep breaths through my nose. Pressure squeezed my sides. I opened my mouth to pull in air. My breathing was ragged, and even though my abdomen rose and fell, nothing was getting into my lungs. I was getting light-headed, my vision dimming. I sat up straighter in the chair, pulled my shoulders back, like Dad told me to do that time I fell off the top of the slide at the playground and landed flat on my back and couldn't breathe.

"Slow and deep, in through your nose, out through your mouth," he'd said, kneeling beside me with his hand resting on my forehead.

I focused on the plant in Mr. Patterson's office and tried Dad's technique. On breath number five, I felt my lungs release and flood with air. I took more deep breaths, then wiped the sweat from my forehead.

I gazed at the test on the table. Words from the story popped out: *family, mother, father, adventure, legacy*. These things were unattainable for me now. I was never going to learn another lesson from my parents, nor was I going to build new memories with them. In the story, the girl convinced her mother to go back to her war-torn country, to find the family left behind. Why couldn't I have convinced my mother to run with me? There was plenty of space under the coop for both of us to hide. I should have argued, but after seven years, I knew better than to challenge my parents. If I had let myself be Zoe, maybe my mom would still be alive.

The walls in Mr. Patterson's office became too confining. I was done and wanted out of this place.

"You're done already?" Mr. Patterson and Mrs. Belkin looked surprised to see me in the door to the office.

"I guess." I shrugged.

Mrs. Belkin took the papers from me, looking at my answers and flipping pages.

"Thanks for coming in to take the test, Zoe," Mr. Patterson said. "Tell your grandmother we will call in a few days to let you know the results."

I gave them both a thin-lipped smile and walked out of the office.

I startled Lottie when I opened the car door and sat down.

"That was fast," she said as she started the car. "How'd it go?"

"It was OK," I said. "There were a few questions that I couldn't answer, but it was mostly easy stuff."

"Maybe they gave you a test that wasn't so hard given, you know, where you came from."

I spun my whole body in my seat to face her. "Why does everyone think I was living under a rock at the commune?" I spat. "We had some very capable teachers. People who went to school to be teachers. They weren't just some nuts who volunteered to teach us. Do you think we scratched our lessons onto chalkboard tablets? That we had Bible lessons every day?"

Lottie glared at me as I yelled. She threw the car into reverse and screeched out of the school parking lot.

"There's no need to talk to me like that. I'm the only one you've got right now. I didn't sign up to parent a teenager, especially one who has been cut off from the world for seven years."

I shriveled into my seat, afraid that if I said another word, she might take me back to Gary. I should have known better than to open my big mouth. It never went well for me when I did that at the commune, so why did I think it would be different now? As I sat there next to this woman I barely knew, I wondered how to fix this.

"I'm sorry," I muttered, looking at my hands. "I'm just frustrated. I know better, and I will be better. I promise. Please don't send me away," I begged. "Please?"

Lottie glanced over at me. She pulled the car off to the side of the road. She sighed, resting her forehead on her hands gripping the steering wheel.

"You'd think by my age I'd know better than to run my mouth off." She looked at me, and the tears forming in her eyes caught me by surprise. "Look, I'm not equipped to process taking in a kid and losing my own at the same time. We both need time to adjust to this new life. I would never abandon you, Zoe. I'm not giving up on you ever again."

She unbuckled her seat belt, leaning over to hug me. I stiffened, and then relaxed into her arms, letting myself feel safe and sure in the space she created for me.

twenty

LOTTIE'S VOICE woke me the next morning.

"I don't know when I'll be back," I heard her say. "We need time. I'm sure Johanna can fill in for me."

She paused, and I realized she was on the phone.

"'K. Talk to you later. Bye."

From the warmth of my bed, I listened to Lottie hang the kitchen phone back in its cradle, fill the kettle with water, then plug it in to boil. Listening to life was a skill I developed at the commune. I could tell from the change of pitch when an empty bucket was almost filled with water. I knew by the lack of echo in my footsteps to the bathroom that our trailer was covered in snow. I could hear how flat Hannah's voice became when she had her monthly cramps.

I burrowed myself deeper into my comforter, wondering who was on the phone. Only now did it occur to me that Lottie might —probably did—have a job. My arrival had disrupted her whole life. No wonder she sometimes seemed so mad. No wonder she was pushing for me to go to school.

The smoky, nutty smell of instant chicory coffee called to me. It was a familiar scent from long before we left. It was hard to believe my grandmother had been drinking the same brand all this time. I swung my legs out of bed, threw a sweatshirt on over my pajamas, and shuffled into the kitchen.

"Good morning," Lottie sang, clearly in a good mood. "Sleep well?"

I rubbed my eyes, picking the crusted overnight goop from the corners. "Yeah, actually. That bed is comfy."

I was surprised how well I was sleeping. I had expected more frequent nightmares. One of the many doctors and therapists who passed through Gary's to check on the kids had said nightmares were an expected side effect of trauma. Maybe I was one of the lucky unaffected few.

"I'm surprised," Lottie said, putting a steaming mug in front of me. "It's almost ten years old." She turned back to the kettle and clicked it on to boil again, even though we both had fresh cups of coffee.

"Well, it feels like it's brand new. If it's that old, it's hardly been slept in."

"It hasn't," Lottie muttered. "I bought it for sleepovers ..."

When I looked up, Lottie was tearing a piece of paper towel off the roll. She wiped the tears from her eyes, then blew her nose. She was shaking her head, like she was trying to wipe away a memory.

Oh. That bed was meant for when Eric or I stayed over. I don't know if my brother ever did. I had a hazy recollection of staying with my grandmother a couple of times.

"Want some eggs for breakfast?" Lottie asked.

I shook my head. "I'm not really hungry. The coffee will do for now. Can I ask you something?"

"Sure."

"Do you have a job?"

"Yes."

"What do you do?"

"I work for an auto parts company. I'm the bookkeeper."

"Do you like it?"

"I've been there for twenty-three years, so if I don't, I'm either too lazy to look for a different job or I have a high tolerance for bullshit."

A laugh erupted from me, and I choked on the coffee I had just sipped. Lottie handed me a paper towel to wipe the brown spit from my chin and the kitchen table.

Lottie decided to make eggs anyway, and the smell of onions frying with the scramble made my mouth water.

"In all seriousness," I said, "I'm sorry if I got you in trouble for missing work."

"I'm not in any trouble. I took some time off," she said, placing two plates on the table before turning back to the skillet on the stove. "I've got one foot out the door, anyway."

"What do you mean?"

"I'm just a few years away from retirement. Maybe now is a good time to shave back my hours." Lottie spooned scrambled eggs onto each of the plates. "Go down to four days a week. Might be nice to have long weekends all the time. What do you think?"

"Um, OK, I guess." I shrugged, unsure why she was asking my opinion.

"We can make Fridays *our* day. Kane Days."

"Isn't there school on Fridays?"

"Around here, high school is only a half day on Fridays."

I stabbed some eggs, dipping them in ketchup. I liked the sound of that. An afternoon off to do whatever we wanted. I especially liked that it was Lottie's idea.

"What would we do?" I asked.

"Whatever the hell we want. Go to the mall. Visit a museum. Drive with no destination. Bake a cake and eat it for supper." Lottie sat down across from me, pulling her plate toward her. "Let's start with the last one." She looked over at me, raising her eyebrows up and down.

"Do we have to wait until school starts?"

"No, we don't. We can start today. So, what will it be? Chocolate or vanilla cake?"

"Vanilla cake with chocolate icing would be perfect. I make the best icing. Everyone says … said so." My stomach clenched. Would all my moments of happiness be shaded with grief?

Lottie reached across the table to squeeze my hand.

"We'll be OK," she said. "Cake won't fix things or make the pain go away for you or me. But we can create something new, just for us."

twenty-one

EVEN THOUGH I barely left the house, most of December went by in a blur. The school called to let me know I would be entering as a sophomore, but with my high score in math, I was going to be placed in junior-level classes for that subject. My education at the commune did not leave me behind at all.

Agents Dan and Shivani surprised us by showing up at the house with news. They had found an underground bunker a little more than a mile from the commune, filled with guns, ammunition, canned goods, water, and other supplies.

We stood just inside the front door, the agents having refused Lottie's invitation to come in and have a coffee or tea.

"There were many bedrooms, a kitchen, a common living area," Agent Miller explained. "Enough space and provisions for a dozen people to live for a year, maybe more."

"I don't understand," I said, shaking my head. I couldn't envision what they were talking about. "Where was this? How could I have not known this existed?"

"We found the entry hatch in what we thought was just a dry river bed. It had been undisturbed for so long that sagebrush and bitterbrush had grown over the entire area."

I knew the plants well. We had boiled and crushed the leaves of sagebrush for medicinal paste. The bitterbrush, when the flowers bloomed, looked like lemon meringue and smelled just as sweet but were bitter on the tongue.

"Wait, did you say a dozen people? There were more than a

hundred of us …" My words drifted away. Maybe Abraham built the bunker a long time ago, when the commune was new and small. My gut told me otherwise.

"Zoe, did you ever hear your father talking about apocalypse, end of the world, stuff like that?" Agent Chopra asked.

Why are they asking me about Dad? I wondered.

I started to shake my head but stopped. I did remember. Mom and Dad talked about it in whispers when they thought I was sleeping. I swallowed my words, not wanting to betray whatever secrets died with my parents. Nothing I could tell the agents would bring my parents back. I shook my head again.

"Well, if anything comes to mind … I'll leave my card with your grandmother."

"Do you know why he did it? Why Abraham killed everyone?" I asked.

Agent Chopra looked down at the notepad she was holding. She was flipping pages, like she was looking for the answer to my question.

"We're still working on that," Agent Miller answered.

"Sometimes crazy just is," Lottie said after they left. "Are you OK, Zo?"

I walked into the living room and sank into the couch, cradling my forehead in my palms.

"Hey, what's going on?" my grandmother asked, settling in beside me and placing a hand in the middle of my back.

"I … I … lied." Tears pooled, then dripped onto my lap. "They did talk about the apocalypse. Mom and Dad. And Abraham too."

I heard Lottie take a short breath through her nose.

"Am I going to be in trouble?" I sniffed.

Lottie circled her hand on my back. I could feel her warmth through my sweatshirt. "No, you won't be in any trouble. It doesn't matter what you know, or what you tell them or not tell them. They'll figure it out because it's their job." She took another breath. "Zoe, do you think the world is going to end?"

I shrugged one shoulder, then shook my head. "I did, kind of, when I was little. It wasn't talked about in Sunday services or in school, but we heard things from the adults when they thought us kids couldn't hear. I didn't really understand it. My friend Hannah and I thought the end of the world was like the end of school."

A new wave of grief washed over me, settling like a boulder in my chest. Fresh tears poured down my face.

"I should have paid attention!" I wailed. "Maybe we could have stopped him!"

Lottie took my chin in her hand and turned my face toward hers. "This is not on you," she whispered. "There is nothing you did or could have done that would have changed anything. You hear me? Nothing."

I heard her, but I didn't believe her. I had spent too many nights wondering what I could have done differently, how I could have saved my parents. I spent just as many nights imagining myself defying my mother and not running away at all, perishing along with everyone I loved.

Over the next couple of weeks, Lottie went to work, while I absent-mindedly surfed television channels. When the weather forecast called for a snowstorm, Lottie hired a chimney sweep to clean the fireplace flue, we ordered some wood, and we hunkered down with rented movies and junk food, the fire blazing, as the snow piled up outside.

All around us, the neighbors had put up their Christmas lights, tethered their inflatables to lawns, erected Santas and reindeer on roofs. Neither Lottie nor I brought up the holiday. I wanted nothing more than to let Christmas pass unnoticed. We did not go to the mall, even though I needed new clothes. I wasn't ready for crowds yet, still fearful of being recognized, but more than that, I didn't want to be reminded.

The first Christmas after Eric died, Dad brought home a tree, but we never decorated it. The ornaments, stockings, and Christmas villages Mom displayed all over the house never came out of the attic. We all drifted around in our sorrow. The tree shed its needles, creating a ring of dried, abandoned death. Two days before my birthday in February, Dad hauled the bare and shriveled thing into the backyard while Mom vacuumed up the needles.

Knowing that Christmas would assault our senses at the grocery store, we planned a mega-shop. The goal was to get everything we needed to sustain us through the holidays so we could avoid going back until the new year. I was able to tune out the carols playing over the store's speakers. I skipped past the aisle filled with candy canes and boxed chocolates. I walked by the poinsettias without issue.

When I wandered past the bakery, the smell of gingerbread nearly brought me to my knees. Mom loved making gingerbread. Even before Eric's cancer, Mom and I would spend the weekend before Christmas baking cookies. My job was to use the cookie cutter and place the little people on the baking sheet. Mom made icing from scratch too, and I stood on a stepstool, squeezing the icing onto the cookies, trying to make sure my gingerbread people didn't look worried or sick.

The world tilted sideways, and I felt Lottie's hand grip my elbow.

"Let's go," she said, a hint of impatience in her voice. She pushed our fully loaded grocery cart off to the side, abandoning it among the dinner rolls and hot-cross buns.

I let her guide me out of the store and into the car. I closed my eyes against the sting of tears, trying to hold them back.

"Stupid, stupid, stupid," Lottie muttered as she climbed into the driver's seat.

I sank back into the rough upholstery, curling my shoulders forward. I just wanted to be invisible. "Sorry," I mumbled.

"For what?" my grandmother snapped.

The tension in her voice was too much for me. I knew that feeling well, of having screwed up and letting people down. As Ruth, I had backpedaled, turning the blame onto myself so as not to make things worse.

"For messing up the groceries. Now we'll have nothing to eat. I can go back in. I'll go get the cart and check out."

Lottie turned in her seat to face me. I kept my eyes on my lap, avoiding the disappointment I was sure to see in her eyes.

"You'll do no such thing," she said. "You didn't mess anything up, Zoe. Why would you even say that?"

I sat mutely, unable to find words.

"Grief is a tricky bitch." She sighed. "And the holidays are especially hard. I'm the stupid one for not anticipating this might happen. You have nothing to be sorry for. I'm the one who owes *you* an apology."

Behind my closed eyes, the tears built, then burst through, flowing freely down my cheeks and dripping into my lap.

"I thought … I thought … I was … doing OK." I hiccupped. "But … I don't … the smell … the gingerbread …"

"I know. I remember," Lottie said, taking hold of my hand. "I've had seven Christmases to learn how to get through the pain. It doesn't hurt any less, but it gets easier to manage. It will be like that for you too, I hope."

Letting go of my hand, Lottie started the car.

"Wait," I protested. "The groceries …"

"I'll come back later. On my own. Let's go home."

I wiped my tears and looked at Lottie. She met my eyes, nodding once.

"I'm glad you found me, Gran."

She smiled and blinked back her own tears.

"So am I, Zoe."

For the first time since Abraham destroyed my life, I felt like maybe my heart would be able to heal.

twenty-two

ON THE FIRST Monday in January, I surveyed the clothes in my closet, realizing I didn't have a lot of choice about what to wear for my first day of school, but grateful for the blandness of what I did have. I chose blue jeans and a simple black sweatshirt, clothes that would keep me warm and invisible. I applied my makeup with Maria's "less is more" warning in mind but then wiped it all off.

As soon as I entered the school on my first day, though, I realized my efforts to blend in were useless. I knew everyone knew. Eyes followed me everywhere. Students huddled in the halls, leaning against lockers, whispering as I walked by.

"She's the one from that cult. Where the guy killed everyone?"

"She's probably crazy."

"Does she speak English?"

"Nice hand-me-downs."

Each comment stung like a barb. I did my best to keep my face neutral, to not let anyone see my pain. And fear. By the time I finally found my locker, the murmuring voices had been replaced by a loud hum in my ears. I hid my head inside my open locker and let grief wash over me. I bit my lip to hold back my tears. How was I ever going to fit in here?

As I made my way to my first class, I kept my eyes mostly on the floor, only occasionally glancing up to see where I was going. In front of me, two students were engaged in conversation, their heads close together. The boy had a mess of curls piled on top of his head; the girl had her strawberry-blond hair pulled into a twist. When they turned the corner, my heart hammered in my chest. In profile, the girl looked exactly like Hannah. I let my eyes drift to the boy and had to choke back my sob. For a brief second, I actually believed I was seeing James and Hannah.

Thankfully, the teachers did not make a big deal about my presence. Each one took my slip of paper that let them know I was in the right room and gestured toward an empty seat. I avoided eye contact while I walked the aisles between the desks. I did the same thing as I moved from class to class.

Not only was I the new girl, but I was the girl they had seen in magazines, newspapers, and on TV almost every day for a month. I was the new girl who might be a little messed up from being brainwashed. I was the girl who had once been exactly like them.

I kept to myself all morning. I listened to the teachers and was happy to discover I was able to keep up. When the lunch bell rang, I was ready for the break, and my stomach grumbled. Moving with the other bodies through the cafeteria line, I tried to figure out what all the food was behind the protective glass shield.

I stared at the woman serving the food, taking in the net on her head and the smears of orange on the front of her white apron. Her lips were moving, but I couldn't hear her over the symphony of voices all around me. She raised her eyebrows and gave me a tight smile.

"Uh, hello? Pick something," a girl's voice behind me pulled me out of my reverie. "Just how damaged are you?"

"C'mon, Sarah, be nice," another girl said. "She's probably looking for a stalk of wheat to chew on."

I blinked my eyes and forced them to focus on the food. There was no way I was going to turn around to face the speaker.

"Burger?" I whispered. It was the first recognizable thing my eyes landed on.

The lunch lady nodded, sliding a shriveled, greasy patty in a bun onto a plate. I moved forward, helping myself to a soda and an apple. The smell of the cooked meat wafted into my nose, and I realized I was really hungry.

I walked into the main hall of the cafeteria, and I swear the volume went down like it does when people are talking about you when you enter a room. Scanning the full tables, I searched for a place where I could sit alone. I spotted a long table with a single person occupying one end and made my choice, moving toward it to sit at the opposite end. But I was stopped by a vaguely familiar voice.

"Holy crap! Is that you, Zoe?"

I turned to my right, trying to find the source of the voice. A girl with thick, wavy brown hair slowly stood, her glossy lips parting a bit.

"I … can't … believe … my … eyes," she said, spacing out each word. "I heard you were here, but I thought it was a joke."

I stared at this girl, taking in the subtle makeup, the perfect white teeth inside the wide smile. She was wearing black leggings, a baby blue V-neck T-shirt with flutter sleeves, and a single gold chain with a golden tassel that hung perfectly from her neck. There was something vaguely familiar about her face, but I couldn't quite nail it.

"Zoe! It's me … Chelsea!"

I stared at her, trying to match this girl to the kid with the crooked teeth who had been my best friend since kindergarten.

"Seriously? How can you not know me, Zoe?"

I opened my mouth to say something, but the only sound that came out was "Urg." Mortified, I turned away and beelined for the now-vacant table I had first set my sights on.

"Clearly, she's a mental mess," I heard one of the girls sitting with Chelsea say.

"Wouldn't you be?" Chelsea snapped.

I sat alone, feeling the eyes of others burning holes into my back. Everything was so different here. I was a fish out of water. The world had moved on without me. The voices in my head—mostly Abraham—confused me. His words had helped me navigate from being Zoe to becoming Ruth, but that was irrelevant now that I was trying to go the other way.

I picked at my burger, not really feeling hungry now. I sat there, alone, sipping my Coke and chewing a warm pickle, wondering how I was going to convince anyone that I wasn't a complete head case, especially when I didn't fully believe that myself.

twenty-three

IT TOOK two days for them to find me. Mrs. Hornich was reading from *Romeo and Juliet* when the screech of brakes briefly pulled her attention to the windows looking out to the front of the school. There was silence for about fifteen seconds and then I heard the slamming and sliding of van doors. I didn't even need to look to know the media was here. I slinked down in my chair, glad my desk was in the farthest corner of the room, away from the windows.

The voices outside grew louder, and I knew they were coming. I pictured the more tenacious reporters moving from window to window, their foreheads pressed up against the glass, hands cupped around their eyes, peering inside trying to find me.

I stared straight ahead, using my peripheral vision to watch the reporters and camera people move past the classroom. Mrs. Hornich was doing her best to ignore the noise. She droned on about the Montagues and the Capulets, pretending the students were listening to her and not desperately trying to see what was happening. As the crowd outside grew, my classmates rose from their desks to press against the windows, forming a perfect wall of protection for me. I took the opportunity to gather my books and slink out of the room.

The hallway was fully abandoned. Everyone must have been in class, trying to figure out what was going on. I stood in the middle of the hallway, not sure where to go. I was frozen in place. Leaving the building was not an option.

"Follow me," a voice drifted from the left.

I turned my head to see Tristan West standing there, his blond hair glowing in the sun from the skylights. We had two classes together, and it took me exactly that long to learn he was one of the most popular kids in school.

I had no voice. I gazed at him with what must have been a stupid look on my face: confusion (*Why are you talking to me*) mixed with appreciation (*Thank you for talking to me*).

"Come on," he urged. "I'm guessing they're here for you."

Tristan gently cupped my elbow, pushing me forward a little. I felt every nerve in my arm come alive, the sensation zip-lining to my stomach.

"I've got the perfect place to hide," he said, leading me down the hallway.

We stopped halfway down the hall, in front of the door to the boys' bathroom. Tristan pulled the door open and nudged me.

"I … I can't go in there." I looked over my shoulder. The halls were still empty.

"That is exactly why you need to go in. No one will think of looking for you in there."

I took a step forward, then stopped.

"What if someone comes in?"

"Just go in the stall, lock the door, and sit on the toilet. It'll look like someone is doing their business. No one will bother you."

It was such a stupid idea it was actually kind of brilliant. The only window in the bathroom was high up in the wall and frosted. No camera lens could penetrate that. What if one of them got bold enough to sneak into the school and search the girls' bathroom?

The bell rang, and the doors to the classrooms flew open.

"Go!" Tristan shoved me into the bathroom, and I beelined for one of the two stalls. I closed the door and turned the latch just as the bathroom door burst open. A few boys came in, laughing and chatting about the chaos outside the building.

"Crazy, huh?" one said. "They're looking for that girl from that cult thing, right?"

"Maybe you should get out there in front of the cameras, Dylan," said another. "Might be your only chance to get on that blind date reality show."

"Will you remember me when you're famous?" another voice teased.

I jumped out of my skin when someone pushed on the door of the stall I was hiding in. As the boy settled in the stall next door, I pulled my books closer to my chest, trying to muffle my thudding heart. I was starting to panic about someone looking under the door and seeing a girl hiding in the boys' bathroom.

I didn't move a muscle. I barely allowed myself to breathe. I waited for the boys to finish and leave. The bell for the next class rang, but no one seemed in a hurry to get there.

It took forever for the bathroom to empty. I waited for the noise from the hallway to die down, then I stood up to unlock the stall when the door opened again. I froze and sat back down on the toilet.

"Zoe, are you still here?" Tristan asked.

I was startled to hear him call my name. I was surprised he even knew it. When I opened the stall, Tristan leaned against a sink, his arms bent behind him for support. Beneath his T-shirt, I could see the outline of his biceps. I looked away, not wanting to be caught gawking.

"It's safe now." He smiled. "I heard Principal Twohig called the cops and they chased every media person off the property. Something about harassment and filming minors without consent. I guess she's good for something other than doling out detention."

"Thanks for helping me," I said, hugging my books tighter to my chest. I couldn't believe how nice he was being to someone he didn't even know.

Tristan shrugged. "I can't imagine what it's like, being followed everywhere you go. You're, like, famous."

My stomach fluttered. Even though it was annoying to be a headline, it felt nice to be in Tristan's spotlight.

"It's no big deal," I lied. "I stopped noticing the reporters and photographers after a while. But I guess they'll be around every time I do something new."

"So that pretty much covers every day of your life now." He grinned.

Fire filled my chest, my legs, and my face. I couldn't even stop my eyes when they fell onto Tristan's smiling, smooth lips.

Lustful thoughts will take you down the wrong path, Abraham said more than once in services.

"Let's get out of here," Tristan said, heading toward the door.

He pulled it open for me and stood behind it, like a gentleman allowing a lady to pass. I locked eyes with him for a second and saw a flicker of something. Admiration? Amusement?

As soon as I was out the door, it became clear to me what shone in Tristan's eyes. Mischief.

"Oh my god! Did she use the boys' bathroom?!" The voice came from directly in front of me. It was Sarah Folk, the girl who taunted me in the cafeteria line on my first day, pointing at me and covering her mouth while she laughed.

Every face in the hallway turned in my direction while mine burned with humiliation. I spun left, then right, unable to focus on where I needed to go to get out of this hallway.

I looked over my shoulder at Tristan, hoping he would come to my defense and explain what had happened. What I saw tore my heart in two. Tristan was standing behind me with his friends, all of them laughing at my expense.

I kept my eyes locked on my feet as I fled, pushing through the bodies. The jeering slapped against my back as I ran to the front door of the school.

"Can you even read?"

"Did everyone share a bathroom where you came from?"

"Go back to your cult, weirdo!"

A few rogue tears dripped and spread onto the tops of my runners. I had been so happy to get these preloved shoes. They were barely dirty when I plucked them off the shelf of the thrift store. Now they would forever be stained with my pain.

By the time I pushed open the door and ran out into the crisp January air, full tears were streaming down my face. I kept moving forward, stopping only when I could no longer see the school. I made my way to a neighborhood lane and leaned against a wooden fence where I closed my eyes and sobbed, not caring if anyone heard me.

Bending over and bracing myself with my hands on my knees, I let everything flow out. I gulped air quickly and made myself puke. I wiped my mouth with the sleeve of my shirt, not caring about the clotted bits of digested breakfast stuck to the fabric.

Eventually, I slid down to sit on the frozen gravel, my sobs ebbing into quiet tears. I cried about my parents, my brother, and about the life I was now stuck in. Stupid Zoe, thinking I could slip back into normal.

When the tears finally stopped, I looked both ways down the lane and knew I was lost. Not just geographically, but inside of me too.

twenty-four

I DIDN'T GO to school the next day. I had barely slept. The nightmares came one after another. If I wasn't fumbling around in a strange place, I was being torn apart by a giant spider or being abandoned in a frozen tundra with a compass that didn't work. And always there was laughter, Sarah's and Tristan's, and even Chelsea's.

I heard Lottie call from the kitchen, telling me to get up. I threw a dirty sweatshirt over my pajamas and plodded into the kitchen.

"I'm not feeling great today. Can I just go back to bed?"

Her eyes traveled from my head to my feet.

"What's wrong?"

"I feel like I need to throw up. My throat hurts."

She pressed her lips together. I could tell she didn't believe me. I silently prayed she would get it and let me skip school.

"Fine," she agreed. "Stay home. I have to go into work for a few hours, but I'll call the school before I go."

"You don't have to call. It's high school. No one cares." I didn't want her calling the office and then have Mrs. Belkin tell her about the media showing up. I wasn't sure if Lottie would let it go or if she would demand the school do something to protect me. I didn't want any special treatment. That would only make things worse.

Before she walked out the front door, she turned, locking her eyes onto mine.

"It'll get better. For both of us. I promise."

I went back to bed after Lottie left, but sleep eluded me. I stared at the ceiling, trying not to replay what happened at school. For the first time in my life, I was utterly alone. *Lottie must be wrong*, I thought, *because I cannot see how anything will ever get better*. The hundred people who were my only family since I was a little kid were now gone. I would never again have a conversation with Hannah. That sweet girl who only ever saw the good in people. Who probably smiled wide before she died, not comprehending why something so bad happened to her.

And the sick thing was, I was kind of jealous. She would never grow up, but she would never know this heartache that was ripping me apart. The grief swallowed me whole, and loss invaded every part of my body. I pulled my covers over my head trying to suffocate the pain. Instead, my brain conjured horrible images of what it must have been like for everyone in those final moments. While I hid under the chicken coop. My envy replaced itself with guilt.

I forced myself to get out of bed, went into the kitchen, and made myself an instant coffee. I flipped through some of the cookbooks Lottie had tucked into the corner by the fridge, hoping to be distracted by pictures of beautiful food. The smoky taste of the coffee was perfect for browsing recipes for cocoa bars, bread pudding, and beef Wellington. The pages of all the cookbooks were pristine, and I wondered if my grandmother had ever cracked one open.

I moved into the living room, staring at the blank TV screen. Sarah's and Tristan's laughter echoed in my head again. If I had just walked over to the windows in the classroom and given the media what they wanted, I would never have followed Tristan into the bathroom. If I had just stayed as Ruth, none of this would have happened.

I went back to my bedroom, tepid coffee in hand, and stared out my small window into the rectangular yard. Lottie had two trees, one in each of the far corners, towering over the house. The elm where the tire swing used to be was naked, stripped of its leaves for the winter. The other was pine, its evergreen needles weighted down with snow. I could tell Lottie took care of this tree. The lower third had been cleared of branches.

We cut back the bottom so the top can continue to grow, Dad had told me when I helped him with his grounds duty. As we walked among the ponderosa pines, lodgepoles, and Douglas firs, I collected pine cones in the pockets of my dress. At home that evening, Dad pointed out the mouse-tail shapes tucked into the folds of the Douglas fir's cone and where to find the seeds buried in the triangular points of the ponderosa cones. Despite Mom's protests, Dad let me use a kitchen knife to cut open the lodgepole pine cone so he could show me the seeds hidden inside.

You can eat any of these seeds, raw, roasted, or toasted, he said. Dad was full of facts and was the smartest person I knew.

As I dropped down onto my bed, I squeezed my eyes. I pictured his face, but it was already getting fuzzy at the edges. I wanted to feel his arms around me, wrapping me in a hug as my feet lifted from the ground. He had been gone for two days, in the community hall for meetings according to Mom, before Abraham went crazy. I can't even remember the last thing I said to him.

Maybe he got away, I imagined, and was now in the forests of Idaho, staying alive by eating pine seeds. Maybe he was hiding, trying to figure out his next move. Maybe, once he discovered the commune was destroyed, he would make his way back to his childhood home. He and Lottie could make up, and we could be a family again.

This was childish dreaming I knew, but I was bored and my

mind was wandering. I second-guessed my decision to skip school. When I shuffled into the kitchen to make another cup of coffee, I caught movement through the frosted glass of the front door. I froze, waiting for the doorbell to ring, and when it did, I tiptoed backward, sliding against the kitchen counter to avoid the windows. I was almost in my bedroom when the knocking started. It was three knocks, then another three.

"Zoe? Are you home? It's me. Chelsea."

I glanced at the clock on the wall in the hallway. She should be at school.

She knocked again.

"Zoe? I saw you moving in there. Please open the door."

I looked down at myself in my too-short pajamas and stained sweatshirt. I reached up to smooth my hair and could feel the grease from not having showered yet today.

I pulled open the door and found Chelsea standing there, bouncing up and down on the balls of her feet, mittened hands clutched in front of her face.

"Can I come in? It's freezing out here."

I nodded, pulling the door open wider for her. As she kicked off her boots, her eyes flicked around the kitchen and into the living room.

"Boy, this place hasn't changed at all since we were kids."

I stared mutely at her, trying to figure out what she was doing here.

"Lottie used to give us bagel chips and spinach dip whenever we came over. I always loved that about her." Chelsea shoved her hands into the front pockets of her jeans. "I used to think it was so cool and ... I don't know ... grown up for us to be snacking like that. Other grandmothers baked cookies or cakes." Chelsea moved her hands to her back pockets. "Does she still have bagel chips?"

Chelsea looked at me, her eyes wide, waiting for an answer.

Something about the way she was standing, with her elbows tucked behind her, made her seem open and inviting.

"I don't know, and I really don't remember any of that." I shrugged. "Do you want a coffee or something? We have instant."

Chelsea shook her head. "No, thanks. I noticed you weren't at school today and I wanted to check on you."

"I'm fine, thanks."

Chelsea followed me into the kitchen, and we sat down at opposite ends of the table. She unzipped her parka but kept it on.

"How are you, really?"

Lonely. Sad most of the time. Feeling like I'll never fit in anywhere.

"I'm adjusting," I answered. "Still trying to figure things out."

She nodded but didn't say anything.

We sat there for a few minutes, listening to the occasional car pass by on the street. My dream came back to me. Chelsea wasn't laughing now. I looked at her face, but she was examining the frosted tips of her fingernails.

"Why are you here?" I asked.

"I told you. I noticed you weren't—"

I cut her off. "Why are you here, really?" I realized I didn't know this girl at all. Neither of us had any idea what the other had become over the last seven years.

"I missed you, you know. It's been hard." She looked at me, tears welling up in her perfectly mascaraed eyes.

A coil of anger snapped inside me. "Harder than watching your brother die and then finding out your parents were murdered?" I lashed out. "That everyone you knew was shot, then burned? I feel bad for you, Chelsea," I snarked, not trying to keep the sarcasm out of my voice.

A cloud of darkness passed over her eyes and her cheeks flushed.

"I wasn't ... I didn't ... I ..."

"You what? You came over here hoping I could make you feel better?" I spat, literally. She flinched as my spit landed on the table in front of her. "Did you want to hug it out? Come on in, Chelsea. I stink and my clothes are gross, but if you want to dirty up your pretty jacket, fine."

"You're messed up," she said, standing and pushing back her chair. "I get that. I would be too if I went through what you did. I came to check on the girl who used to be my best friend. I can see she's gone now."

"Yeah, that's ancient history."

Chelsea crossed her arms in front of her chest, then dropped them to her sides.

"I don't believe that. You're still in there, Zoe."

I stayed at the table, looking at the scratches on its top. Chelsea silently pulled her boots back on, hesitating at the front door before she pulled it closed behind her.

twenty-five

MY HEART FELT like it was shattering into a million little pieces. I rubbed my palm across the left side of my chest, trying to massage away the pain. I could breathe just fine, but the space above my breasts felt like someone had used it as a punching bag. I sat up on my bed, propped pillows behind me, trying to make the pain go away. I lay down again to see if that made any difference. I sat up, swung my legs over the side of the bed, and bent over at the waist. My head hung between my knees, my hair falling over in front of me. I waited for nausea to rise. I could feel the blood rushing to my head. My brain pulsed, trying to push itself against my forehead. I was hyperaware of every nerve in my body.

Breathing while bent over was getting hard. My breath caught in the back of my throat when I tried to choke back my sobs. I was glad Lottie wasn't home to witness this, me sounding like a seal choking on a too-big fish. I cried and I cried and I cried. I wanted the sadness and struggle to pour out of me. But it wasn't working, and that made me cry even harder.

When I had no more tears and pain left to release, I lifted my head and my body. Too fast. The blood rushed up and my brain filled with anguish again. My life was in ruins. *You are worthless*, I told myself. *Undeserving of love*. Why was I still here? My family was fading from my mind. I could see my mother's smile and then she was pulling away from me, like she was in an ocean being dragged out to the horizon. I wanted to be with my family again. I wanted the good life I had when I was Ruth.

There was a black hole swirling inside me, sucking the last remnants of my happiness into its gloom. I didn't have the energy to fight anymore. I had been fighting for so many years at the commune, and I lost anyway.

I closed my eyes, imagining what I'd be doing if I was at the commune right now. Hannah and I would be finishing our home-work, and then we'd wander over to clean out the horse stalls in the barn. It would take forever, because we'd have to pet all the horses, whispering our secrets in their ears and to each other.

I'd muck horse poop forever if it meant I could be with my parents again.

My mouth filled with saliva and my stomach was queasy. I raced to the bathroom, but when I bent over the toilet, nothing came. I spit my saliva into the bowl, then sat on the edge of the tub. My hands rested on my thighs, palms up. My face was tight from the salt of my tears. I looked at my hands, letting my eyes follow the blue and purple branches of my life snaking up my arms. On my right wrist, a vein pushed itself up, a tributary of life that said "I'm here, waiting and ready."

And then, I was rooting around in the cabinet under the sink, throwing things out in a rage. I yanked out rolls of toilet paper, rusted tins of scouring powder, fragrant bars of soap, a crinkly bag of cotton balls. A bottle of mouthwash. Tampons and pads. Discarded and mismatched rubber gloves. Kneeling, I reached into the shadows at the back, when my hand landed on some-thing papery. I couldn't grip it, so I used the tips of my fingers to shuffle it forward.

When it came into the light, the translucent paper revealed the wavy cuts in the center of a razor blade. I gingerly opened the packet, folding the edges of the paper away to find three unused blades. They must have belonged to Grandpa Jake.

Still on my knees, I was surrounded by abandoned hygiene products. I rocked back on my heels and then sat down, knocking bottles and boxes out of the way. I settled on the cool tile of the floor with the razor blades in the palm of my hand. The edges gleamed in the light. I plucked one from the paper, carefully holding it from the center to avoid cutting my fingers.

I contemplated what ending my life would do to Lottie. I bargained with a god I'd never seen. I argued with the girl I wanted to be. I had no reason to keep on living. I had every reason to take my own life.

I placed the sharp edge of the blade on that bulbous vein on my right wrist. I tilted the blade, placing the slightest pressure on my skin. My flesh crinkled, but there was no cut yet. I added more pressure, squeezing my eyes shut. I didn't want the last thing I saw to be the toilet. I called James to mind, my first crush, and imagined his face moving closer to mine, leaning in for a kiss. I could see the fullness of his lips. I could smell the candied grapes he loved to eat. I took a small breath, more of a gasp, preparing myself for this, my first kiss. He was almost there, his lips puckering to meet mine.

At the last second, James was pulled away by some invisible force and replaced with another: Tristan. He erupted into laughter. Bodies and faces blurred in my peripheral vision, and everyone laughed at me. "As if," Tristan whispered into my heartbreak.

One swipe up. That's all it would take to end this. A single stroke, deep and meaningful and I'd never have to deal with anything ever again. I could wipe away Abraham and not spend another minute wondering why he wanted us all to die. I was one vein away from reuniting with my family in the afterlife, if such a thing existed.

I opened my eyes, since I needed to see what I was doing. I pressed down harder. A small dot of blood beaded up from under the corner of the blade. I pressed again and started to pull it over my skin. A small red line was left in the blade's wake, but it didn't look like anything worse than a surface scratch.

I lifted the blade from my wrist.

In a fog, I put everything back. I rewrapped the blades, tucking them behind a bottle of hand lotion. I turned on the water in the tub, letting the water rush over my right hand and wrist, rinsing away any evidence of what I had failed to do. I was alive for another day.

twenty-six

I FELT Lottie's eyes on me the next morning as I moved around the kitchen, making myself an instant coffee and getting a bowl of cereal. I did my best to give off a "Don't talk to me" vibe. I kept my head down and did not make eye contact.

My grandmother leaned against the wall next to the fridge, arms crossed over her chest. I stole a glance at her face. Her mouth was a thin line, and her chin was thrust forward. I'd seen that look on my dad's face at the commune whenever I was in trouble.

"Excuse me," I snapped as I reached for the fridge door. "I need to get in there."

Lottie threw her hands up in the air, a dramatic surrender, and moved to the other side of the kitchen to lean against the stove.

It was freaking me out, how she was just there, not saying anything. She stood like a painted portrait whose eyes follow me everywhere. I pushed back the shiver, replacing it with more anger.

"You can't hide out here for the rest of your life. You need to go back to school," she said.

The message was clear. There was no way she was going to let me stay home for another day. I also knew there was no way my repeated absence was going to make everyone at school forget I existed. I was going to have to face them at some point. And I'd made everything worse by being a complete jerk to Chelsea. The one girl who could have been an ally.

"What's got you so pissed off today?" Lottie asked.

I glanced at her as I shrugged.

"Have you lost the ability to speak?" I could hear the sarcasm in her voice.

I kept silent. It was the only way I could control myself.

"Let me ask you something. Was this kind of behavior acceptable in the commune? How were moody teenagers handled? If you were there right now, what would Ruth do?"

That was all it took for me to explode.

"If I was at the commune," I spat, "none of this would be happening. My parents would still be alive. I'd be with my friends. Life would be normal."

"Normal? There was nothing normal about how you were stolen from me. How you were taught to be. This attitude? This one right here?" She pointed a finger at me and waved it in the air, tracing my body from head to toe. "This is the Zoe I know. All this fire and fight is who you are, who you've always been. You are not built to be quiet and cooperative all the time. You've convinced yourself that Ruth was who you wanted, or needed, to be."

I turned my back so she couldn't see me roll my eyes. I took a sip of coffee, savoring the bitter sting of caffeine and heat.

"I'm not your enemy, Zoe. I'm your family. I know who you are."

"I'm that weird girl from the cult. A brainwashed, Bible-thumping weirdo," I muttered.

Lottie pushed herself away from the stove and walked to me. She put her hands on my shoulders, guided me to the kitchen table and pushed me down into a chair. She sat across from me.

"Is that why you've ditched school?"

I looked into my mug and nodded.

"Want to tell me about it?"

I looked up at her and blinked back my tears. I was so tired of crying all the time.

"It's all horrible. The reporters showed up. Someone was nice to me, but it turns out I was part of a big joke. Everyone laughed at me. Then, I had a fight with Chelsea. I thought if I … I tried … Bad things aren't supposed to happen to me. To Ruth."

Abraham had promised us that. *When you are agreeable and follow the rules, you invite fulfillment into your life.*

"Bad things happen no matter who you are." Lottie sighed. "I'm sorry to say this, but you will always be that girl who survived that tragedy at the commune. You've got to figure out who you want to be. It's OK to be unsure. You'll fail at some things and thrive at others. Kanes are not quitters. We always rise."

"My dad quit. And he took us all with him."

"He did what he thought was best for his family. I still haven't forgiven him for taking you away from me." She shook her head. "The same blood that makes us fighters makes us hold grudges."

"Is that why you missed my birthday party?"

"I have no reasonable excuse for that. When Eric died, I crawled into my own hole. I did that when your grandpa passed too, and your father never forgave me for not being able to help him through his grief."

Grandpa Jake died in his sleep when I was four. The only memory of him I managed to hold on to was how sad Dad had been. For what felt like forever, Dad was lost, hardly talking or eating. Even at four, I could sense the grief Dad had in his heart.

"Why didn't you get married again?" I asked my grandmother.

Lottie sighed, heavily. "Your grandpa was the great love of my life. He was my best friend. When they lowered his coffin into the ground, I tried to throw myself in there with him. That kind of thing spreads quickly in social circles. Everyone thought I was off my rocker."

"Seems I'm not the only Kane who's a headcase," I joked. I held my breath, waiting for Lottie to tell me off, kick me out, or lecture me about being ungrateful.

"Yeah." She chuckled. "And I didn't have to shovel chicken poop and get brainwashed to earn that title. Did that all on my own."

I stood up and walked over to where she sat, wrapping my arms around her back. I squeezed my grandmother in a hug.

"Thank you for that," I said.

"Would it help if you had someone else to talk to? Maybe that Dr. Zaretsky can suggest someone local?"

I nodded. "I'll think about it. But for now, I think I know what I need to do."

I went back to my room to dig through my dresser and closet. When I first got here, I had put my stuff away without really considering how things worked together. Now, as I pulled out item after item, I discovered there were some cool things in there: deliberately torn jeans, fitted tees, short dresses with flirty hems—all items I had been taught were immodest and would never have been allowed to wear.

I assessed the array of donated clothing, accessories, and shoes, and realized I had no idea how to put any of these things together. I needed help, and the person most qualified to help was probably not going to talk to me at all.

Difficult tasks usually require difficult choices, Abraham had always been fond of saying. Until this moment, I hadn't really thought about what that meant. At the commune, most decisions had been made for me.

If I wanted to change my look, if I wanted to ditch the image of Ruth who wore clothes that concealed, I was going to have to do something Ruth would never have done. I was going to have to be bold and ask for help. I had to work out how to apologize to Chelsea. Would she even listen to me?

The phone in the hallway between the bedrooms sat on its own table, its yellowed and coiled cord twisted by time and use. I hadn't used a phone in more than seven years.

Chelsea's was the first phone number, besides my own, that I had memorized. I lifted the handset from its cradle and nestled it between my ear and my shoulder, closing my eyes and trying to remember the sequence. I held my breath as I pushed the buttons, wondering if the number was the same after all these years. With each number, the phone chimed in my ear. Then a click before it connected and the ringing started. Once, twice. From where I stood, I could see the clock on the wall in the kitchen. It was just past seven o'clock in the morning.

In the middle of the third ring, Chelsea's mom picked up.

"Hello?"

"Hi, Mrs. Elklund?"

"Yes?"

"It's … Zoe. Can I talk to Chelsea, please?"

"Zoe! I am so pleased to hear you are back home. We've missed you around here. I am so sorry for your loss. My heart is broken—"

I heard Chelsea's muffled voice in the background. "Mom, give me the phone. Hello? Hi?"

"Chelsea … I'm … I … I'm really sorry about what happened yesterday."

There was a pause, and I wasn't sure if she was still on the line. I was about to say something again when she spoke.

"I'm sorry too. I guess we were due for a big fight. Our last one was, like, what, ten years ago?"

"What?" I asked.

"The last fight we had? I guess you don't remember. It was after I pushed you into the pool with all your clothes on."

I closed my eyes, trying to recall that day. I had a fuzzy memory of feeling the weight of my soaking wet clothes.

"I can't even remember why I was so mad."

"Oh, I do." Chelsea giggled. "I ruined your lip balm."

"What?"

"You had that lip balm ball. The one that had just the slightest bit of color for your lips. I had wanted one for, like, forever, but my mom wouldn't buy it for me. *Your* mom let you get one and I was jealous. So, after you put it in the front pocket of your jeans, I pushed you into our pool."

A rush of sadness washed over me, and I had to lean against the wall. My words choked in my throat, and I fought to not cry. Now it was my turn to pause.

"Zoe? Are you still there?"

"Yeah," I whispered. I forced out a cough to clear the shaking in my voice.

"Do you … should I not talk about your mom?"

I was about to answer her, telling her it was still too new, but I realized she was the only one who held memories of my mom that weren't tied to death. I needed her to remind me how good things used to be.

"That's OK, actually. Can you come over before school today? I need help with putting together what to wear. I've got all these clothes here, and I don't know what goes with what. I have no idea what's, um, cool."

"You don't need me to come over, Zoe. There are no rules other than this—dress like you made a deliberate choice. I can tell you what looks good, what I'd wear, but that's not the same as what you'd wear. Just pick some things you like and see how they make you feel."

"Umm, OK. It's been a long time since I had clothes to choose from, and I don't know …"

Chelsea sighed. "Wear whatever you like, Zoe. People are

going to be jerks no matter what your clothes look like. If you're stuck, throw on some jeans and a top. Keep it simple."

"Thanks, Chelsea. See you later?"

"Sure. Um, Zoe?"

"Yeah?"

"I'm really sorry about what happened outside the boys' bathroom. I'm sorry I wasn't there to defend you. I'm a crappy friend."

I didn't know what to say. My Ruth instinct was to apologize for her discomfort, but the Zoe part of me knew that was not my problem.

"We're all just trying to figure things out," I finally said.

"Yeah. Hey, do you want to eat lunch with me and my friends today?"

"That would be great."

When I hung up, I smiled, but part of me was nervous about sitting in the crowded cafeteria at a table with people I didn't know. All eyes would be on us, on me.

There were two pairs of jeans on my bed. One had random rips up and down the legs, the others were a deep indigo blue. Those were the ones I picked up and slid on. I chose a bright yellow top with buttons down the front, short sleeves, and an elasticized hem at the bottom. The delicate eyelet cutouts in the top half of the blouse ran from the shoulder to just below my neck. I stood in front of the mirror, shocked by what I saw. The jeans hugged my legs but sat slightly loose at my hips. The bottom of the blouse rested right above my waist, revealing a thin line of flesh. I gasped and blushed at my own body.

At the commune, we wore shapeless dresses, loose shirts, and pants. Modesty and functionality were the rule. Anything that gave the slightest view of skin, other than ankles, forearms, and neck or sat too close to the body was burned in a naming ceremony.

I turned away from the mirror and sorted through the other shirts on my bed. I found a long, flowing dark green tunic. I switched out the blouse for the tunic and felt much more comfortable. The tunic hung to the middle of my thighs, concealing everything.

I gazed at myself in the mirror. In these clothes, I was safe. I could move freely, I could hide, I could blend into the background. I sat on my bed, still looking at my reflection. My eyes drifted to the eyelet blouse, then back to the mirror.

Chelsea was right about people being jerks. I could proceed with caution, exactly what Ruth would do. Or I could let my Zoe flag fly and be bold, show some skin, and own it. Be deliberately confident. Drive the conversation in a different direction. Be a Kane.

I changed back into the blouse, pulling the hem up above my belly button. I didn't care that it was cold outside. It didn't matter that the jeans clung to my legs. I piled my hair into a messy bun on top of my head, then swiped a faint rust-colored eyeshadow on my eyes. I shaded the outside edges of my lids with a dusting of brown, just like Maria taught me. I applied my eyeliner and mascara. Then I stood in front of the mirror, fists resting on my hips, and straightened my spine. I wasn't sure if I could pull this off, but I had to try.

Look out, world. Zoe's back.

twenty-seven

WHEN I STEPPED out of the house, the January air tickled the inside of my nose. I shivered, wrapping my brand-new wool coat around me. I had fallen in love with this coat the moment I found it. It was dark gray, with embroidered green vines and pink flowers snaking their way from each cuff to the shoulder. I rubbed my thumb over the silky threads and immediately decided I had to have it. Lottie warned me it wouldn't be warm enough for the bone-cracking cold of a Montana winter, but I didn't care. I had prayed on bare knees in the bitter sting of an Idaho blizzard; I could layer my clothes under the looseness of the coat.

"A Kane would never wear something like that." Lottie laughed.

"Says the lady who wears purple socks inside her boots." I smiled.

I was enjoying the quiet walk through the neighborhood when the rumbling of the school bus came up behind me. I was anticipating rude shouting out the windows, but the kids on the bus didn't know new Zoe was beneath the boiled wool. I kept my chin up, playing out smart comebacks in my head, ready to fight. When the bus rumbled by without incident, I was relieved.

I strutted to my locker when I got to school. As I took off my coat, I glanced around me, hoping someone would notice my new look. I saw someone do a double take, and I turned my face back to my locker, hiding the smile playing across my lips.

"Oh … my … gawd! Zoe!"

I turned to see Chelsea and two of her friends standing in the middle of the hallway. One of the girls was chewing gum and blowing bubbles, taking me in from head to toe. The other girl's mouth hung open. Chelsea's whole face was lit with a smile so wide I could see her molars.

"Hey," I said, trying and failing to hide my own smile.

"Turn around. Give me a circle. I want to take in the whole look."

I threw my arms out to the side and twirled.

"I know what's missing," Chelsea said.

She reached into her crossbody purse, pulling out two tubes. She moved toward me, and I took a step back.

"What is that?"

"Lip gloss. That face and that bod"—she pointed to my head and then my chest—"absolutely require a finishing touch. Please, please try this."

She handed me the tubes. One was a soft, almost nude pink and the other shone like metal ribboned with blue, green, pink, and yellow. I handed the muted color back to her.

"Go big or go home, right? Got a mirror?"

Chelsea dug into her purse again and fished out a compact mirror. I applied a single coat of gloss, first to my top lip, then the bottom. I could smell vanilla and something sweet like candy. I pressed my lips together and they stuck. It felt weird for a second, but when I looked in the mirror, I understood why Chelsea loved this stuff. My lips looked fuller than they ever had, and the color brightened my skin.

"Wow," said one of the other girls. "That color looks amazing on you."

"Yeah," agreed the gum chewer. "I'd totally kiss those lips."

There was a second of awkward silence, then laughter erupted.

"Selfie?" Chelsea asked.

I put my hands up in front of my face. "No. No more media."

"This new look is going to bring them back, you know," Chelsea said. "I can see the caption: 'Cult girl gone wild!'"

"Please don't use that word," I whispered. I felt Ruth stirring, trying to find a way to hide and retreat. I pushed that frightened and meek girl aside, raised my head, and stepped into the girl I used to be.

"It wasn't a cult," I explained. "It was my home. I was a kid, going to school and hanging out with my friends, just like you, Chelsea. The only thing that was different was the geography." I gently closed my locker and looked her right in the eye. "And it's all gone now."

Chelsea paled. The other two girls had their eyes glued to the floor.

"Zoe, I … I'm sorry," she stuttered. "I didn't mean … I don't think you're crazy or anything … I was just joking around. Like we used to."

Something clicked in my brain, like a puzzle piece sliding into place. Chelsea didn't know who I was now any more than I did. We were both stuck with memories of who I used to be. With a blinding clarity, I realized I needed Chelsea's help to fit into this life. She was the thin thread connecting me to who I was becoming before my family left. It was a tie I couldn't afford to cut.

"That's OK," I assured her. "I know you weren't trying to be mean. It's an ugly word, though. My commune life was mostly simple."

"Maybe one day, you'll tell me about it?" I could see the pleading in her eyes.

I nodded, and she threw her arms around me, squeezing me in a quick hug.

"I'm glad you're back," she whispered in my ear.

As I walked to my first class, the whispers started again, but unlike my first day, this time the voices were not taunting me. These were the kind of comments I could handle.

"Is that Zoe? She looks amazing."

"She cleans up nice."

"That outfit is fire!"

By lunch, I was floating on air from all the nice attention. Chelsea waved me over to her table in the cafeteria to join her, Mya, and Tori. They chatted about boys, girls, teachers, and dreams for the future. I didn't have much to say. I smiled and nodded at what I thought were the right times. I was happy to be in their company and tried to follow the conversation.

"Does it make you uncomfortable that I'm a lesbian?" Mya asked me.

"Why would that bother me?"

"Isn't that, I don't know, like, forbidden, where you came from?"

"Mya! Really?" Chelsea huffed.

"It's OK." I sighed. "We weren't purists."

"I thought all those kinds of places were anti-everything not biblical," Tori said.

I shook my head. I looked down at my sad school-supplied sandwich wrapped in plastic. I really didn't want to talk about this, but if I didn't, then I left the conversation in the hands of the rumor mill.

"Only our names were biblical," I explained. "Yeah, we prayed, but we made up our own prayers. We had sermons on Sundays, but it was more so the whole community could gather and be together."

"I heard on the news that all the women and girls had to dress the same. Isn't that kind of cultish?" Mya asked.

"Not to me. It was practical. The men and boys all wore the same pants too."

"Ugh, I would die if I had to wear the same thing as everyone else," Tori whined.

"Tori," Chelsea hissed, widening her eyes before flashing them over to me.

"What?" Tori asked, not immediately realizing what she had said.

"Maybe be a bit more sensitive about the words coming out of your mouth," Chelsea said through clenched teeth.

Tori's brow furrowed. "What are you talk—" The light bulb went on. "Oh, shit. I'm sorry, Zoe. I didn't mean … I mean, I wasn't—"

"It's OK," I said. I leaned my shoulder into Tori's, giving her a friendly bump. My desire to blend in and move forward was getting stronger than my grief. "You know, now that I think about it," I continued, "there are a lot of names in the Bible. I was the only Ruth out of more than a hundred people."

"There's at least six Victorias in this school," Tori said. "I thought going by Tori would set me apart, but turns out, three of us use that nickname."

"You know how to stand out? Survive a maniac." I paused, enjoying the moment of power. I looked across the table at Chelsea and winked. Then we all burst into laughter.

"Well, well," a boy's voice came from behind me. "Is this another new girl?"

Tristan plopped himself on the bench beside me, turning his body to assess "the new girl."

"Holy crap! Zoe? You look … so … so different."

My face turned instantly red. I was torn between enjoying the attention and hating him for the horrible thing he did to me.

"Thanks," I said, doing my best to look anywhere else but directly at him. The sting of humiliation was still strong.

"Look, I'm sorry about what happened a few days ago. I didn't really mean anything by it."

"It was a jerk thing to do, Tristan," Chelsea said.

"Can we start again?" he asked me.

"Why would she do that?" Chelsea snorted, not giving me the chance to answer. "What makes you so special that she'd want to be friends with you?"

My eyes flicked between the two of them. Tristan shifted on the bench and for a split second, I felt his thigh pressed against mine. I jerked my leg away, not wanting any kind of contact.

"It was a prank, Chels. You've played one or two on me. But I don't hate you for it."

Chelsea crossed her arms over her chest and scrunched her brow. She glared at Tristan, and I watched the indecision change her face. With every piece of my being, I wanted her to take my side, but Chelsea and Tristan had a history I wasn't part of. Best friends can't stay that way when one disappears for seven years. My absence set the expiry date for our friendship.

"Nope." She shook her head. "That was beyond just a prank, Tristan. It was mean and unnecessary. You can go now. Bye." She flicked her hands at him, waving him off.

Tristan turned to look at me. "I really am sorry, Zoe."

I met his eyes and saw the pleading there. *Sometimes people do things out of their own pain that hurts others,* Abraham lectured once. He urged us all to be forgiving, but I was done with being a doormat for someone else's issues.

"I accept your apology, but I'd like to eat lunch with my friends. Maybe one day, you can sit with us. But not today, Tristan."

He rose from the table and left. Chelsea smiled widely.

"And that, Zoe, is what we call a burn." She giggled.

We were full-on laughing when the bell rang.

twenty-eight

BY THE TIME the snow was mostly melted and the promise of spring was in the air, I had become the fourth in Chelsea's group. I found my groove in school. Bit by bit, I had shed the commune, fully embracing my life as the resurrected Zoe Kane.

Apparently, I had what Lottie called a "fluid personality." I shifted from group to group. I could be friends with those who loved science just as easily as I could be friends with anyone who loved art. I could see the questions in people's eyes. They wanted to ask me about the commune, but it's not the kind of thing that naturally comes up in conversation. So, I led people there. I decided that if people wanted to gossip about me, it would be with the right information. Whenever I saw someone looking at me, a question on their lips, I opened the door and invited them in. I offered the answers to the questions they were too embarrassed to ask. No, I wasn't molested; no, I wasn't brainwashed; and there were no creepy rituals.

In class, I confidently raised my hand to participate. I dug into my homework, I studied for tests, I did all the required reading. My grades climbed higher, and I aimed to keep them there.

I stopped taking the bus in the morning, preferring the refreshing early-morning walk. At the front doors, I would run into the athletes, including Fynn, Marco, and Tristan, who had apologized daily for a month before I forgave him, and they all made the same joke.

"Our cheerleading squad of one has arrived!" Every single

morning. And I laughed, even though it was no longer funny. As I made my way to the library—either to study or read something for fun—I smiled to myself, happy in what was shaping up to be a perfectly normal life.

One early morning I sat on the floor in front of my locker while Tristan and Marco sat on the floor across from me, watching a video on Marco's phone.

"Hey, are you coming to the party this weekend?" Tristan asked me.

"What party?"

"The midterm party? At Fynn's?"

"It was a text invite," Marco said as I shook my head.

"I don't have a phone."

"How do you survive without one? That's like being cut off from the world," Marco said.

Tristan elbowed Marco hard. Marco gave Tristan a dirty look, then looked over at me.

"Oh, shoot, Zoe. I'm sorry. Sometimes my mouth just fires off without my brain." He knocked a palm to his forehead. "Stupido."

"It's OK." I shrugged. "No big deal." I didn't think they were trying to be mean. They had forgotten who I was and where I had come from. And that was actually a very good thing for me.

"You should come to the party," Tristan said. He opened his binder, wrote something down, tore out the page, and slid it across to me. The paper glided across the dingy linoleum and stopped right in front of my crisscrossed legs. A perfect shot.

On the paper was a time and address.

"For the party?" I asked, feeling stupid the second the words came out of my mouth.

Tristan nodded.

"It's on the other side of town. New neighborhood." Tristan smiled.

I smiled back, grateful he didn't make fun of my confusion.

"OK. Great. See you then."

"You mean, see you second period in English." He laughed as he rose and walked away.

"You should come," Marco said, turning to me after he closed his locker. I folded the paper and slid it into the back pocket of my jeans. "Fynn's pool parties are legendary. Something crazy always happens."

I raised an eyebrow. "Isn't it too cold to swim?"

Marco threw his head back and laughed. His black curls bounced along with the rest of his body.

"At Fynn's, anything goes. See you there, newbie."

I watched Marco walk away, getting swallowed up by the sea of bodies filling the halls before the first bell rang.

At lunch, I asked Chelsea if she was going to the party.

"Of course. Are you … are you coming?"

The words flew out of my mouth before I could stop them. "Tristan invited me."

I saw a shadow flicker in her eyes. Tori sipped her soda, turning her head to look at Chelsea beside her on the bench. Mya froze with a gravy-soaked French fry on the way to her mouth. She sat beside me, oblivious to the brown liquid dripping onto the table.

"He … invited … you?"

The way Chelsea said it, with a mix of surprise and disappointment in her tone, made me realize she liked Tristan. I felt like I needed to explain myself.

"Not like, invited me, like as a date or anything. He just asked if I was going."

"So, are you going?" Tori asked.

"I think so. Are you guys going?"

They all nodded.

"Do you want to come with us?" Chelsea asked. "I'll pick

you up." Chelsea had turned sixteen on the third of January and got her driver's license the very next day. When my own birthday came the following month, I hadn't been ready to try driving yet. There had been plans for a birthday party, but when the media started sniffing around, pushing out stories about my "'bitter'sweet sixteen," I opted for pizza and a movie in Tori's basement along with Chelsea and Mya.

As I walked home after school, I couldn't stop myself from smiling. Fynn's party would be my first high school event. But by the time I got home, my brain was in worry overdrive. Would there be new people I didn't know? And even though we were all friends, part of me worried they might be planning another joke. I got stuck between desperately wanting to go and being terrified that I was going to be the target.

But I had to go. Of course I did. It would be high school suicide not to.

When Chelsea got to my house Saturday evening, Mya and Tori weren't in the car.

"Are we going to pick them up?"

"Nah, Tori's mom is driving them. We'll all go home together, though."

"Thanks for coming to get me."

Chelsea turned her head to look at me, long enough that I was nervous about how long her eyes had been off the road.

"I wanted to talk to you alone."

My palms started to sweat, even though it was cool in the car. No good conversations ever began that way.

"What's up?" I asked, trying to hide the quiver in my voice.

"What was it really like?"

"What was what like?"

"Living in a commune."

I wasn't sure why she was asking. Did she think I was hiding something? I turned my head, examining Chelsea's profile. In the years I was gone, her face changed shape. It was longer now, her chin more pronounced. I realized that even though we were best friends once, I didn't really know who this girl sitting behind the wheel had become. The last time we shared a ride, she was sitting on the back of my new bicycle. A lot had happened between streamers hanging from the handlebars and crystal beads hanging from the rearview mirror.

"It was fun once I got used to the idea," I said. "I thought we were just on vacation. We were staying in a trailer, and there weren't a lot of rules. There were bonfires and I got to stay up late. It was like a dreamworld for an eight-year-old."

"That sounds like summer camp," Chelsea said.

"It wasn't. At all. We changed our names. All the stuff we brought with us was burned. I thought I was being punished for Eric's death."

"Oh my god, Zoe. I am so sorry …"

I was looking out the side window as we drove down Main Street, taking in all the signs for spring sales on the storefronts. We were both quiet as we passed through and until we were in the residential area on the other side of town.

"Do you remember when we went to the summer fair and dressed up in Victorian costumes for a photo?" I asked, turning to look out the windshield.

"I do!" Chelsea squealed. "That was so much fun. The guy in the kiosk let us try on almost everything he had. And it was so hot that day. Everything was sweaty when we were done."

"How did we not know how gross that was?" I laughed.

"Right? Those costumes probably never got washed."

"Do you still have that photo?" I asked.

"I think so." Chelsea nodded. "Probably buried somewhere in the chaos of my closet. Do you still have your copy?"

"I did." I sighed. "Until it was burned."

Chelsea didn't say anything for a while.

"Was it all horrible?" she whispered, breaking the silence.

"Not at all," I protested. "There were things that were weird, like being in the same classroom with kids from all grades. But I learned a ton of things I probably never would have. I know how to mend socks and pluck a chicken. I can build a fire with a few twigs and dried leaves. I know what plants are safe to eat and which ones will make you sick for days. My parents were so happy being there. It was good for them. Until it wasn't. I'm sure the plan was to live there until the day they died. None of us thought it would happen so soon."

"Or the way it happened," she whispered.

We sat in silence for the rest of the drive. There were so many cars on the street, we had to park two blocks down from Fynn's house.

"Can I ask you another question?" Chelsea said as I opened my door.

I had one leg already outside the car. I nodded and waited for her to speak.

"What was it like, being Ruth?"

I pulled my leg back in and closed the door.

"I was just a kid like anyone else," I answered.

"No, I mean, did you have to be someone totally different?"

All the time.

"At first, it was like playing dress-up. It was fun to pretend to be someone else."

"But that changed?"

I nodded. "After a month, I wanted to be Zoe again. But it couldn't happen. I had to learn to live as Ruth."

"Was that hard?"

"Very. I made some terrible mistakes. It was so hard to be Ruth all the time," I told Chelsea, "but I practiced, taking little bits of Zoe out of me, day by day."

"I'm sorry to say this, but what a bunch of assholes," Chelsea seethed. "That's a crappy thing to do to a kid."

I snorted. "Yeah, but it's not like I had a choice."

"No, I guess not." Chelsea sighed. "Do you feel you were brainwashed?"

I shook my head. I had talked about this for hours with Dr. Duxelles, my new therapist. She explained the difference between brainwashing and conformity, then let me talk out where I thought I landed.

"No. Maybe. I don't know. I mean, I always felt like Ruth was just a uniform I put on but could never take off. If I'd been brainwashed, wouldn't I have changed everything I thought and believed?"

"Can we ever truly change who we are?"

"That is way too deep of a conversation for a Saturday night." I chuckled. "But short answer? No. I always felt like an impostor."

Chelsea's hands were still gripping the steering wheel. She flicked up the fingers of both hands, examining her frosted pick manicure.

"Isn't that like every teenager everywhere? You're not that special, Zo." She turned her head to look at me, and I saw a familiar glint in her eye.

"Screw you," I shot back with a grin. "Who else do you know who is a sole survivor? Show me anyone else here who lost her entire family." I still held the grin, but my insides squirmed.

She pressed her lips together, squinting at me. "I know you're trying to act like you don't care, but the Zoe I once knew screamed her feelings for all the world to hear. Do you remember after your brother's funeral?"

I closed my eyes and leaned my head against the headrest. I

had been feeling a million things that day, but all I could get a grip on was my anger.

"Your hands were shaking so hard, you spilled soda all over your dress. You went off the rails about that."

"Yeah, but it wasn't about the drink at all," I admitted. "I was so mad at Eric for dying. He stole my parents from me, and it was all for nothing." I knuckled away the tears from the corners of my eyes. "And now it happened again. My parents have been stolen from me forever."

"I'm so sorry, Zoe." Chelsea reached over to lay a hand on my shoulder and squeezed. "I'm still here for you, like I was back then."

We had been sitting in the car for so long, every window was fogged. Before we got out to make our way to the party, I traced ZK into the dew.

twenty-nine

THERE WERE SO many people packed into Fynn's house. Some were familiar to me from school, but as anticipated, there were a lot of faces I didn't recognize. As we walked through the crowd, I tried to ignore the whispers and the subtle pointing in my direction. Chelsea became my shield. I stuck close to her as we made our way through the living room to the kitchen where we helped ourselves to cans of soda.

"Can I offer you a cup of liquid sunshine?" someone behind me said.

I felt a tap on my shoulder, and there was Tristan, blond hair sticking out from all sides of his head. He was holding out a cup with an unnaturally bright green liquid inside.

"Nice hair, Tristan," Chelsea said, taking the cup I thought he was offering me. She made a face as she sniffed it.

"You like?" He winked. "It's my party hair."

"That's a thing?" she asked.

"It is if you want it to be."

Chelsea rolled her eyes.

"What's in this?" she asked, holding up the cup.

"Lemonade," he answered.

"And …?"

Tristan shrugged and raised his eyebrows. "I honestly have no clue what you're talking about." He smirked.

Chelsea sniffed the cup again, then put it down on a coffee table.

"I'm driving. So, I'll pass on whatever this is. C'mon, Zoe, let's find Mya and Tori."

We found them in the backyard by the pool. Since it was only April, the pool was still covered with a protective plastic sheet. The music from inside the house was playing on speakers placed at intervals around the pool deck. A gazebo with two couches and a pair of chairs sat off to one side, lanterns hanging from its four corners. String lights were draped on the fences, giving the whole backyard a warm, comforting glow. This would be a great place to hang out all summer.

For the next couple of hours, I could not wipe the smile off my face. We danced in groups. We drank so much sugary soda I thought I might puke. I watched people pair off and slink away. I eavesdropped on conversations and was pleasantly surprised whenever I was asked to share my opinion.

At some point, I drifted away from Chelsea, Mya, and Tori, moving through the house, having conversations with people I had only passed in the school halls. I had long ago stopped automatically searching faces, hoping to see one of my friends from the commune. As I wandered back to the pool, listening to the music and laughter, I realized that most of these people didn't care—or know—that Ruth existed. To them, I was just Zoe.

Through the din, I heard a familiar voice coming from the lounge chairs on the far side of the pool. I felt removed from my body as I walked in that direction, as if pulled by some unseen force. As I got closer, I saw Marco and Tristan sitting side by side on loungers, faces lit by the screen of Marco's phone.

I thought I heard Abraham, and it stopped me in my tracks. I held my breath, straining to hear. Then a female voice came from the phone, sounding like it was coming through a tin can.

"While we may never know what really triggered the murderous rampage, police have said they discovered videotapes that clearly show the members of the commune were descending

into madness. Please note, some of the footage we are about to play may be disturbing to sensitive viewers."

And then I very clearly heard my father's voice.

"Is it so wrong to want to be happy? I just want to be free—don't you? We all have that right. The outside world is coming for us. The danger is closing in, trying to crush us with their oppression. I—we—can't just sit here like pigs waiting for slaughter. We have to take our fate into our own hands."

Abraham's voice played through the phone next. *"The only ones you can trust are those who truly love you. I love you. In the next life, you will find peace. You can throw away all the lies you've been told. You can be free of your pain."*

The newscaster cut in. *"A computer salvaged from the ashes held documents referring to the end of the world, the apocalypse, and the insurrection," the reporter continued. "The FBI now has evidence that the commune's leader, Joshua Morris, who called himself Abraham, and his accomplice, Stephen Kane, who changed his name to Reuben. The bodies of both men showed signs of suicide.*

A gasp escaped my lips. Tristan looked up and, seeing me frozen there on the pool deck, elbowed Marco. Marco clicked off the phone. Chelsea had followed me out to the pool, but I hadn't even noticed.

"Zoe? Are you OK?" Tristan asked as he rose from the lounger and walked toward me.

Everything I ate that day threatened to come up. The world shimmered around me. Chelsea gently placed her hand on my back, and I leaned into her. My legs were like rubber, and I was sure I was going to fall. Tristan took my elbow and together they guided me to a chair.

"My … my … dad …" I stuttered. I shook my head, trying to rid myself of the thoughts flooding my brain. "The plan all along was to kill us all? My dad was part of that? Oh my god, oh my god …" I put my head in my hands, covering my eyes. I couldn't hold back the wail that built from deep in my chest and forced its way out of my lungs.

"Party's over," Chelsea yelled. "Fynn, please kick everybody out."

Everything after that was a blur. I cried and screamed until my throat was raw and I started coughing. I was handed a cup of water. Something soft and warm was draped over my shoulders.

I stopped when I was emptied of all emotion. I felt hollow and numb. The thick clouds in my head lifted and my thoughts cleared again. Dad *had* been more absent the last couple of years. He came in and out of the trailer at weird times in the middle of the night. He was hardly home for dinner. On one of those rare mornings he was at breakfast, I asked what he was doing that kept him away, and he growled that it was none of my concern. By then, I knew better not to challenge him or any adult in the village.

As I replayed the last seven years of my life in my head, I realized all the lies Abraham told us about the evils in the world outside were his way to control us. He was making us weak-minded and unlikely to fight back. Every word that came out of his mouth was measured and brought every person in the commune closer to death. And my dad went along with it. Helped plan it. Betrayed what was left of our family.

I knew why my mother told me to run.

Despite any rules I had broken and the pressure to be something I wasn't, I was always going to be her daughter. She wasn't going to witness the loss of another child. She told me to run and hide because she wanted me—Zoe, not Ruth—to live.

thirty

BY THE TIME Chelsea took me back to Lottie's, the resolve I had to continue living was not nearly as strong as when I'd left the party. I heard my once and again best friend tell my rediscovered grandmother what had happened, but their voices came through like cotton balls had been stuffed into my ears. My entire body was breaking down. My head was pounding, and my cheeks and my mouth stung like I had wrapped them in barbed wire. I was itching from my shoulders to my torso. When I lay down on my bed, I pulled up my shirt, fully expecting to see an angry, blistering rash. But all I saw were my ribs poking out from the smooth flesh. *I'm still too thin*, I thought, a relic from the scarcity we sometimes had to live through at the commune.

We starved for nothing.

My hips and legs felt disconnected from each other, and I was numb from my thighs to my feet. Except for one spot that burned. The scar on my ankle from climbing the tree felt like it was on fire, but I didn't move to check. I took comfort in the searing pain. It was a bridge between my past life and this one, my way to feel what everyone in the commune must have felt as they burned. I was alive. I could feel. My mother saved my life. I would never be able to forget that I was the only one left.

I crossed my hands over my chest, imagining myself in a coffin. My parents would never get that peaceful burial. Eric had a beautiful funeral, but Mom and Dad were ashes, left to blow away on the first breeze.

My fists clenched at the fabric of my T-shirt, trying to squeeze the fury out of me. How did I not see that Dad was so weak? I spent so much time trying to win his approval, proving myself worthy of his love that I couldn't see he was too bound by his own grief to give me what I needed. A father who helps plan murder is incapable of love.

Again, my rage flared.

How could he be OK with letting me die? How could he give up on us after Eric died?

There was a soft knock at the door, and Lottie poked her head into the room. I don't know what she saw in my face, but she retreated without saying a word.

My father had been my first hero. He picked me up when I fell from that tree, cleaning the deep cut while Mom called the doctor to find out if we should go to emergency. Dad held me in his lap, applying pressure, while we watched the kids' channel on TV. He was always a happy guy, making lemonade out of lemons. Even after his worst day at work as a plumber, the one when a fountain of human shit rained all over him, he laughed as he stepped into the shower fully clothed. And then Eric died, and all the joy was bleached out of him like dying coral.

I rolled onto my side, catching my reflection in the mirror above my dresser. My eye makeup had pooled in the hollows under my eyes, darkening the bags already there. I was a mess, outside and in. How was I going to face everyone at school? By now, all the people at the party, and probably everyone in school, would know that my own father had planned to put a bullet in my head and let me burn.

I needed to know if Lottie knew.

I shuffled into the kitchen, finding Lottie standing at the stove, stirring, her face engulfed in steam.

"What is that?"

"Beef and barley soup. Want to try it?"

I nodded. Lottie took a spoon from the drawer, scooped some out, and then blew on it.

"Um, I'm not five," I teased.

"Some habits die hard." She shrugged.

"I thought you couldn't cook?"

"Oh, I still can't. This is from a package. All I do is add broth, water, chuck, and my special ingredient."

"Which is …?"

"A splash or two of red wine. Now, go sit at the table and I'll serve you a bowl of serenity."

As soon as the bowl was in front of me, the smell lifted some of my sadness. A memory flickered at the edge of my mind, of sitting in this kitchen, my legs dangling, slurping soup. Eric was still alive then, but spending more time at the hospital, as were Mom and Dad. Back then, as now, Lottie made the effort to feed my soul.

"I heard the news." Lottie slid into the chair across from me with her own bowl of soup. "Can we talk about it?"

I slurped but didn't answer.

"I imagine you feel the same as I do. Angry. Embarrassed. Disgusted. Betrayed. Am I right?"

I sat back in my chair, mirroring my grandmother. She put the right words to everything. Her lips were pressed together, her arms placed flat on the table.

"How could he do this?" Tears flooded my eyes. I let them loose.

"I don't know, Zoe." She sighed. "I didn't raise him like that. Something broke in him when Eric died. I tried to help, as any mother would for her child. But I couldn't reach him. Losing his father unexpectedly and then losing Eric … I guess it was too much for him to handle."

"But he still had me," I cried. "I still needed my dad. He.

Still. Had. Me." I pounded my chest with each word. The dam burst and we were both crying now.

"How could he value my life so little?" I wailed. "How does a father plan to murder his own daughter?"

"We will never know why he did what he did." Lottie used the palms of her hands to wipe her tears. "There are no answers that will ever take away this pain. We can hurt together, Zoe."

Lottie reached across the table, pulled my hands away from my chest, and squeezed them.

"We are still here. I am still here. We'll get through this."

I pulled a napkin from the holder on the table and dried my cheeks.

"How can I face anybody at school?" I squeaked. "What if the reporters show up again? What am I going to do?"

"You're going to ignore everyone. Walk with your head high. This was a choice your father made, not you. You have nothing to be ashamed of."

"That's not how high school works."

"I know I may seem ancient to you, but I remember what it was like. The times have changed, but people are the same. Your friends will stand by you. Pay attention to that. Everyone else can go to hell."

I leaned forward, inhaling the comfort from my bowl of soup. I couldn't hide forever, I knew that. As I slurped and chewed and filled my stomach with warmth, I felt the broken pieces inside me drift together. I could do this. Abraham led my father down a terrible path, but I had Lottie as my lighthouse. No one understood as well as she did. I wasn't alone. With every spoonful, I was starting to feel whole again.

thirty-one

LOTTIE WAS RIGHT. The following Monday, there were no reporters lurking about trying to get a photo or ask questions. At school, my friends formed a human shield around me. Chelsea glared at anyone who dared to whisper anything within earshot. Mya and Tori were glued to my sides. Tristan and Marco brought up the rear. Their athletic bulk was enough of a warning to anyone who was considering slinging any mud.

I quietly pushed through the day, trying to concentrate on what the teachers were saying. In my geography class just before lunch, the intercom speaker burst to life. "Mr. McMurty, can you please send Zoe Kane to the office at the end of class?" Every student turned in their seats to look at me. My face burned.

"Maybe those Hollywood people are here for you," Sarah Folk whispered, a huge grin lighting up her face. "They want to start filming your reality show. Or more likely, the aliens have come to take you home." She laughed.

I collected my textbook and binder, put them in my knapsack, then flung one strap onto my shoulder.

"Best of luck in the looney bin." Sarah snickered.

"Maybe later you can give me some advice about what it was like," I shot back. Her grin vanished and she glared.

With my head held up, I walked out of the classroom and made my way down the hall. When I got to the office, the secretary waved me into the principal's office.

"Come on in," Mrs. Twohig said, motioning for me to take a

seat in the only empty chair in front of her desk. Mr. Patterson occupied the other seat. It felt like I was about to be ambushed. As the principal shuffled some papers around, I examined her face. Her eyebrows weren't scrunched together like when she had to deliver stern news. Her lips were curled into a slight smile, like she was going to enjoy whatever she had to do. I could only hope that she was going to tell me she was expelling Sarah and her friends, the same girls who called her Mrs. TooThick.

"Miss Kane," she said, "I'm sure you have no idea why you are here, so I'm going to get right to the point. You've got the highest grades in all your classes. That is remarkable given where you … came from."

Mr. Patterson nodded along as Mrs. Twohig spoke. "We also know—and hear—there have been some, uh, challenges adjusting to the social circles," he said.

Oh. My. God. Are they actually going to talk about this? Please, please, don't make me talk about my feelings. Don't ask me to snitch out the bitches. That will only make things worse.

"We all feel like you need an opportunity to come out of your shell in an environment that is different from the halls of this school," he said.

My head turned from Mr. Patterson to Mrs. Twohig and back to Mr. Patterson.

"I don't understand," I said, trying to make sense of what they were saying. "Are you … am I being kicked out of school?"

Mrs. Twohig laughed, then handed me a pamphlet. "Not at all! We want to send you to a leadership summit."

I stared at the trifold in my hand. The front page had a picture of teenagers sitting in a circle, their faces frozen in laughter and smiling like they didn't have a care in the world. Emblazoned above the photo were the words *The Green Valley Leadership Foundation*.

"What is this?" I asked.

"It's a four-day conference for teens. We've been sending one sophomore every year for the last twenty years," Mrs. Twohig explained. "We think this would be a great thing for you. This has nothing to do with recent revelations. I want you to understand that."

I opened the pamphlet, scanning the contents. Words popped off the page. *Values. Leaders. Excellence. Integrity. Empower.*

"Um, I think you have the wrong person. This doesn't sound like me at all."

"Not yet," Mr. Patterson said. "But I think spending four days here will be life-changing. It's a good foundation for building the skills that are important for the future."

"I think I've had enough experience in the life-changing category, thanks," I said, placing the pamphlet on Mrs. Twohig's desk.

Mr. Patterson leaned forward, pushing the smiling teens back toward me. "OK, maybe that was the wrong choice of words. Zoe, if you want to change what people believe about you, you have to change what you believe about yourself. You are smart and tenacious. You've overcome a horrible experience and yet you walk these halls every day feeling like you don't deserve any better. At least, I think you do. If I'm wrong, please correct me."

I looked down at my lap, not knowing what to say.

Mrs. Twohig sat back in her chair. "You are a survivor, Zoe, and I don't mean that just in the literal sense. I've seen thousands of students come and go through this building, many of who had troubling stories. We want you to go to the leadership summit not as punishment, but as a reward for your academic performance."

"It's amazing what you can do when you are granted a little freedom," Mr. Patterson added. "Four days away from here could be very liberating."

My face got hot. I didn't need a mirror to tell me my cheeks were bright red.

"Do I have to go?"

"No." Mrs. Twohig shook her head. "We've submitted your name to the foundation as our representative, but that's not a commitment that you'll be there."

"Is there someone else who can go if I don't?"

"No," she said again. "We only ever submit one name. To be honest, we've never had a student not want to attend."

"Look," Mr. Patterson said, "we can't force you to go, and we certainly don't want to guilt you into going. This is 100 percent your choice. It won't cost you or your grandmother anything. You just pack a bag and go."

I was seriously torn. I wanted to go but was afraid to. This was the first time in ages I was more than just that girl from that cult. It felt good to be recognized and acknowledged for something else for a change.

I took the pamphlet and left the office with a promise to Mrs. Twohig and Mr. Patterson to think about it. Instead of heading to my next class, I headed for the library. I sat at one of the computers and typed the website from the back of the pamphlet into the browser.

The Green Valley Leadership Foundation was a global organization, with retreats held all over the world. The website was peppered with photos of students among their peers, in earnest conversation, leading an activity, dressed in costumes, and with painted faces.

Could I do any of those things? My palm grew clammy over the curve of the mouse just thinking about going. The thought of people watching me, of having to pull myself out of the invisibility of a crowd, was terrifying. What if I was recognized? What if there were more Sarahs than Chelseas? I'd be stuck there for four days, with nowhere to hide.

As I wiped my hand on my jeans, I heard a voice whisper inside my head.

There is no need to run anymore. You know who you are.

The voice was my mother's, as clear as if she were standing right beside me. I closed my eyes, wanting to hold on to that sound forever. I placed my left hand on my right shoulder, wishing I could feel the warmth of her fingers under mine. I massaged the bones and muscle there and became aware of the throb of my pulse in my fingertips, reminding me I still had a lot of living to do.

thirty-two

WHEN I TOLD Lottie about the retreat, she was adamant that I attend.

"It will be a great opportunity," she said, "but I understand why you don't want to go."

We were in the backyard, cleaning out the last bits of winter in the garden. As I dragged a thatching rake over the grass, my grandmother picked rotted leaves out from the plant beds.

I was so torn about this retreat. Part of me—the Zoe part—was excited to go and stay somewhere else and be part of something great. But Ruth wanted to stay home, where she was safe from the judgment of others.

"I'm really nervous about meeting new people," I confessed. "What if everyone knows who I am and that's all they talk about?"

"So?" Lottie said, picking up a pile of leaves and dumping them in the paper yard waste bag. "You've been through this before. And you'll go through it again. Think of it as an opportunity to change what people think they know."

"But some people's minds can't be changed," I protested.

I was thinking about Sarah Folk, who never stopped tormenting me. She teased me in class, in the cafeteria, and did her best to knock me on my ass in gym class.

"You can't waste any energy on those kinds of people. I've told you before—it's their own insecurities they can't handle. Show compassion and pity instead of trying to prove yourself."

I dropped the thatching rake on the ground and went over to Lottie. I wrapped my arms around her back and squeezed her from behind. I felt her stiffen, then relax.

"I'm happy you found me," I said, leaning my head into her shoulder.

My grandmother turned around and wrapped me in her arms. We stood there, neither of us letting go. We were both very different people from when she came to get me from Gary's place. I had started to feel safe again.

"You're going to this retreat, Zoe, even if I have to drive you there myself."

I laughed as I pulled myself out from the hug.

"OK. Fine. I'll go. But I think I should take the bus like everyone else."

At 6 a.m. the following Thursday, Lottie drove me to the pickup spot at the mall. The parking lot buzzed with students and their families. The bus had not yet arrived, but duffel bags and suitcases were gathered in a massive pile. I rolled my own bright blue suitcase to the expanding collection.

When the bus pulled into the lot, I was surprised. I had expected a yellow school bus, not a sleek silver one with tinted windows. The brakes hissed as the bus came to a stop.

"Well, I guess this is it," Lottie said. "You're going to be fine. I promise."

As we hugged, I looked around at the other kids, also hugging their families. There were high fives and some tears. I felt my own tears threatening to fall.

A voice broke out over the din.

"Good morning, everyone! My name is Jackson, and I'm one of the facilitators this weekend."

I craned my head to see him. He wasn't much older than any of us, but he carried the confidence of someone who was comfortable being in charge. He stood in front of everyone, shoulders back, a wide smile on his face. He pushed off his sunglasses and rested them on top of his short, curly brown hair.

"We have assigned seats on the bus," he said. "I'll call your name and your seat number. Numbers are on the armrests."

"Numbered seats?" Lottie said. "That's fancy. What ever happened to the hot, bouncy, noisy school bus?"

"I was thinking the same thing." I laughed.

We stood awkwardly, listening to Jackson call names and numbers, watching the goodbyes and embraces.

"Zoe Kane, seat forty-two."

I turned to Lottie, who threw her arms around me for another hug.

"Have fun," she said into my hair. "You have the potential for greatness, kid. Remember, you're a Kane."

I squeezed back, giving her a peck on the cheek. I pulled myself away and walked the five steps up to the interior of the bus. I found my seat close to the back and at a window. At least I'd be able to watch the world go by.

It took another half an hour for the bus to fill. Every time someone stepped on, I held my breath, watching as they walked down the aisle searching for the numbers on the armrests.

I stared out the window, watching the parents wave blindly at the tinted glass. Lottie had already left. She didn't like long goodbyes with me.

I felt a puff of air brush against my arm, and I turned my head. Sitting in the seat next to me was a girl with a head full of long copper curls.

"Hi." She smiled. "I'm Shandra. What's your name?"

I paused. This was the moment when I could say anything, be anyone.

"Zoe," I said, lifting my chin.

"Ooh, great name!" She squealed. "Are you not SO EXCITED for this weekend? I cannot believe we get to go. Can you even?"

I stared at her. I had no idea what she was asking me. Before I could open my mouth, she exploded with energy again.

"This bus is really posh. Is that a TV up front? What kind of music do you like? I like almost everything. Except for throat chanting. My dad likes that, but I need words to sing. What school do you go to? I'm at St. Clement's. What is—"

Shandra was cut off by Jackson's voice coming over the bus speakers.

"Welcome aboard! We're going to leave soon, so I want to cover some ground rules. No eating on the bus. Water only. There's a bathroom at the back. We'll arrive at the center in a little more than two hours. When we get there, another facilitator will greet you when we get off the bus and you'll be assigned rooms."

"Ooh, wouldn't it be wild if we were roomies?" Shandra chirped. When she turned her head away from me, her curls bounced off my cheek.

Jackson made final announcements before he sat down in one of the front seats, but I didn't hear a word he said. I was watching the other kids, moving from one side of the bus to the other, shouting and waving goodbye to their loved ones outside that dark glass. As we slowly departed from the parking lot, I watched the parents' eyes, all of them unfocused and unsure where to look.

Shandra plopped back down in her seat.

"This is the first time I've ever been away from home. It feels weird. Have you ever been away from your family?"

I turned away from the window to give her a good look at my face, waiting for the recognition. Even months after what happened, even after the media stopped following me and digging for stories about Abraham and the commune, a day didn't go by when someone didn't know who I was.

"Oh, I get it," Shandra said. "You don't have to talk about it. I'm being nosy. Sorry. One of my quirks. I'm going to miss my bed. I'll miss my dog most. Listen to me … I sound like I'm leaving for months instead of four days. Can you tell I'm a noob?"

I blinked my eyes more times than was necessary. I scanned her face, but I couldn't read what she was thinking.

"So, what should we talk about? Oh, I know! How did you get to be invited to this retreat?"

Shandra lifted her whole body from the seat, then sat down again with her legs crossed. She turned her sparkling blue eyes on me, and I wondered if she was waiting for me to adjust my own seated position.

"I … um … I earned the top marks in my grade," I answered.

"Oh, wow! I certainly didn't do that. At my school, we had to write an essay on an environmental issue but from an opposite position. I wrote about recycling and why it's not the solution to managing waste over the long term. It was hard to write. Not the essay part. I'm kind of good at that. The arguing the other side part. It was hard for me to argue against something I believe in, know what I mean?"

I nodded, having no clue how to respond.

Shandra was doing just fine carrying on the conversation by herself. I could sit here, nodding and smiling.

"So, what do you do for fun? That's a super cool sweater, by the way. Where did you get that?"

"I, uh … I …" I fumbled for words, not sure which question to answer first.

"Seriously, girl, you have some amazing fashion sense."

The laughter erupted from me before I could contain it. I was laughing so hard, my stomach started to hurt. Shandra smiled at me and then she laughed too.

"Fashion sense?" I snorted, when I finally was able to breathe again. "I think you need glasses." My sweater, a thrift shop find, was a V-neck with sleeves that hung loose at my wrists, not by design but by being stretched out from use. The body was light blue, and the sleeves were a deep royal blue.

"My eyesight is perfectly fine," Shandra said as she crossed her arms. "I might not be popular, but I know style when I see it."

"Uh, OK."

"Can I tell you a secret? Something not a lot of people know about me?"

She didn't wait for me to answer.

"I love thrift shopping. My friends and I go once a week. It's our extracurricular activity. One afternoon per week we make the rounds at all the stores."

I grabbed Shandra's arm.

"I LOVE thrifting too! My grandmother and I go, but not every week."

"It's fun, right? It's a treasure hunt to me. You never know what you'll find."

"It used to bother me that my clothes came from there, but now I've kind of embraced that what I wear never looks like what everyone else bought at the mall. Can I tell *you* a secret?"

Shandra lifted her body out of the seat with her legs still crisscrossed and resettled to face me. I mirrored the action, so we were now face-to-face in our seats.

"Tell me," she whispered.

I leaned closer and I could smell lavender in her hair.

"The best day to go is—"

"Tuesday!" she exclaimed at the same time.

We started laughing again. A bloom of happiness warmed my chest. I realized I wanted to keep talking.

We had only been on the bus for a little more than a half hour. For the rest of the journey, we talked about our best thrift finds (hers, an Armani blouse for $8; mine, a trench coat for $4); our schools (she went to an art school on the other side of the city); and the foods we liked. She didn't notice when I shrugged off topics like movies and music. The more we talked, the more I wondered if I had found the only person in the world who didn't seem to know I was that Idaho Massacre Girl from the commune.

We laughed at videos she showed me on her phone. She pulled her backpack from between her legs, and we snuck jelly-beans she'd hidden in there. She was completely oblivious to who I was. It was the best ride of my life.

thirty-three

WE FILED off the bus into the parking lot of the conference center, shielding our eyes from the sun. As we waited for our luggage to be pulled out from the belly of the bus, Shandra put her arm across my shoulders, giggling in my ear about which boys she thought were cute. I laughed along with her, caught up in the glow of new friendship.

As we gathered inside the lobby of the center, another bus arrived in the lot. Shandra pulled me to the large windows at the front to watch. We made up a game where we tried to identify fellow thrifters. She was so much better at it than I was. She knew all the current looks and labels.

There had to be a hundred students gathered in the lobby. Shandra and I managed to find two unoccupied folding chairs, but people sat on the floor and on the tables. Jackson had told us to wait here for instructions and room assignments. Shandra was busy chatting up everyone who was sitting around us, while I took it all in.

The lobby ceiling was made of wood planks painted white. It brought the noise down in the space while making it feel larger than it was. Chandeliers hung throughout the room. All were made of gnarled antlers and were simultaneously cool and hideous.

I was still unsure about being here. My nerves were on edge. I remembered what Mrs. Twohig and Lottie both told me: This will be good for me. I can spend time with like-minded peers. I can stretch my wings a little.

I watched Shandra, with her bouncy hair and bubbly personality, easily engaging in conversation with kids she just met. I wished I had that confidence. When Shandra dragged me into the chatter, I was fine. But I realized I would probably never be someone who would introduce myself at the start. I'd never had to. Where I'd been and who I was announced itself the second I was recognized.

For the next forty-five minutes, I felt like I belonged. I trailed Shandra like a dedicated puppy, while she lapped up the attention. We were talking and laughing with two other girls about trees when the air in the room shifted. I glanced up, toward the front door, thinking maybe some more students arrived or our group leaders were ready to assign rooms.

It wasn't that at all. I should have known this would happen. When I glanced around the room, people were watching me. Heads were coming together in a whisper conspiracy. Chins and eyes shifted in my direction. Some kids were even bold enough to point.

I shuffled behind Shandra. If I didn't look, if I avoided eye contact, maybe this would all go away. I tried to hide my face behind my hair, hoping that people would think I looked a little like that girl, but not enough to be firmly identified.

Shandra was happily ignorant until a boy walked over to us and asked, "Aren't you that girl from the cult?"

The room went completely still. I looked at the floor, hoping it would open and swallow me whole. Shandra glanced over her shoulder at me before looking at the boy.

"Who are you talking to?"

"Her," he said, pointing a finger in my direction. "You're her, aren't you?"

Shandra cut me off before I could speak. "Excuse me, but it's rude to point. Didn't your mother teach you that? Besides, we are here to become better people, to learn to be leaders. It doesn't matter who we are or where we come from. Zoe is my friend, and she's been through hell and back. Leave her be. Please."

My overwhelming desire to hug the life out of Shandra was tempered by the shock of hearing she knew who I was.

"Shandra," I whispered in her ear, "it's OK. Thank you."

She ignored me, putting her hands on her hips, waiting to be challenged.

The guy threw up his hands in surrender and backed away.

"Sorry," he muttered. "No offense."

The damage was done. I felt the eyes in the room burning holes through my skin, like a million embers from a campfire. No matter how much I wanted to be Zoe, Ruth would be remembered.

"It'll be OK," Shandra said. "What happened to you doesn't have to define you."

Before things could get worse, Jackson and his co-leader, Mandy, walked into the room, clipboards in hand, giving them instant authority. By some miracle of fate, Shandra and I had been assigned as roommates.

"How come you didn't tell me you knew who I was?" I asked once we were in our room.

"Because it didn't matter." She shrugged. "Also, I saw a girl on the bus who was going to need an ally ... someone who could understand what she was going through."

I stopped unpacking my suitcase, underwear in hand, and stared at her.

"What?" I asked.

Shandra put the T-shirts she was holding into the top drawer of the dresser we would share. She sat on the bed she had claimed, crossing her legs. I did the same on my own bed.

"OK," Shandra started. She stared at me for a second, then

she looked off to the side. I saw her eyes glaze over and knew she was now locked away in a memory.

"Here goes. I haven't talked about this for a long time." She blew a puff of air through her lips. "When I was ten, I was in an accident. At my tenth birthday party, actually. My parents rented a small yacht, and I invited eight of my best friends for a sleep-over. One day and night on the ocean. It was the best birthday ever. We anchored in a harbor for the night. We tried to stay up late, but the motion of the ocean made us all sleepy. I woke up in a hospital six weeks later. Faulty electrical caused an explosion on the boat. My dad and I were the only survivors. I was clinically dead for almost an hour. So not only am I the girl whose friends and mom died at her birthday party, but I am also the miracle girl who came back to life."

"Holy shit," slipped through my lips before I could stop myself.

"Yup. I was messed up for years. Still am. I'll never get over that loss, and neither will you. And we don't have to. I blamed myself for my mom dying. I wondered why I was the only one of my friends to live. Sometimes, I wish I had died that day too. Do you ever feel that way?"

"I feel one of those things almost every day."

"No one gets what it's like to be the one left behind. We stopped celebrating my birthday after that. My dad crawled into himself and couldn't be a parent. I spent a lot of time hating myself. I couldn't handle the pity looks and the hateful glares."

I wiped away the tears tickling my cheeks.

"I'm so sorry that happened to you. How did you get through it? How can you be so happy?"

Shandra pushed the sleeves of her hoodie up to her elbows and flipped her arms over to show me the underside. There, from her wrists to her elbows, were the faintest of white lines, ghosts of the blades she had used to try to relieve her pain.

"I was barely eleven when I started cutting. I had a teacher who cared and noticed and called my dad. I was in therapy in less than forty-eight hours."

This was far too heavy a conversation to get into. I was starting to feel tired and picked my nails nervously. I thought about sharing my attempt to end my own life, but I held back. I heard my mother's gentle voice: *Sometimes there is more value in listening than talking.*

"How do you get over it?" I asked again.

Shandra shrugged. "I didn't. I deal in my own way. It's easier for me to be happy than to brood. There are for sure days when I want to hide in my closet and cry. I lost all my friends in one day, and for a long time, kids were afraid to be my friend. People will forget, eventually. One day, the world won't remember you were Survivor Girl. *You'll* know it every day, though. In the pain you feel in your heart. Or the need to tell your best friend something, then realizing she'll never pick up the phone. Or when you really, really need a hug from your mom, but you'll never smell her shampoo again."

We were both crying now. I reached out across the gap between our beds to take Shandra's hand. Behind our tears, we were connecting in our grief, marveling at how the two of us found each other. Shandra and I both had mascara running from our eyes like black rivers. We cleaned ourselves up and made our way back to the lobby where the afternoon activities were starting.

When Ms. Twohig invited me to attend this retreat, I thought she'd made a mistake. I didn't want to come, but if I had to, I was ready to absorb what was happening around me, as Ruth had so many times. I'd do what was asked of me. In all the scenes playing out in my head, I never imagined I'd walk arm in arm with a girl who was turning into a friend.

thirty-four

DAY one of the retreat ended with ice-breaker games, some welcome speeches from the facilitators, and a tour of the facility, taking us everywhere inside and out. They showed us the dining hall and kitchen, the library, and meeting spaces. Outside, we toured the reservoir and gardens behind the complex. The place was a mix of modern and farmhouse: the wood-framed and leather furniture in the central hall set against a floor-to-ceiling fireplace of gleaming quartz and metal; an entire wall of windows highlighted the shadows thrown by what I hoped were fake animal heads and antlers. I felt small in all the spaces, dwarfed not only by the décor but also by the larger personalities of the other kids, Shandra included. Over the course of that first day, *What are you doing here* was on replay in my brain.

After breakfast on day two, we were broken up into our groups. My heart flipped when I was separated from Shandra. She tried to calm my nerves by telling me that I didn't have to answer to anybody and to tell people I wasn't at this leadership convention to gossip about the commune. I nodded in agreement, but I knew I would try to be invisible and hide behind my hair.

Before we were sent off to the first activity, Jackson and Mandy gave a little speech about what was going to happen over the next few days.

"This retreat isn't about what we can't do," Mandy said. "It's about discovering what we are capable of. Until we are tested, we don't know what kind of leaders we will be. This weekend is about collaboration and cooperation. Push yourself to your limits. Step out of your cone of safety. This is a safe place to take risks."

For our first activity, three groups were gathered in the central hall. My group of seven sat on the floor in a semicircle. Our leader, Lennox, introduced himself. I couldn't take my eyes off him. His black hair, in locs tied loosely behind his head, trailed down to the middle of his back. His eyes were so green, I thought maybe he was wearing contacts.

"The first question I always get is 'Were you named after the boxer or the furnace?' And my answer is always the same—it doesn't matter, because wherever I go, I bring the heat!"

He tried his best to hold a stern look on his round face, but his lips pulled back from his teeth in a smile that reached his eyes. The other kids giggled and groaned, but I had no idea why. While my education on the commune had been excellent, I still had gaping holes in things that were common knowledge to others.

"This is my tenth year with the leadership camp, and I hope to be here for ten more. I'll be your contact for the whole weekend. We'll have one group session every day, and everything is outlined in these packets."

Lennox reached behind him for a pile of clear blue plastic envelopes the size of a school binder. When I got mine, I could see an itinerary on top. I popped open the button and pulled it out. Almost every hour of the entire weekend was scheduled. Lectures, presentations, and social activities.

"There will be plenty of time to go through your packets later," Lennox said. "Right now, we are going to go around this circle twice. The first time, I want you to introduce yourself. Tell us your name, where you're from, and something you're super proud of."

One thought whirled in my mind: *Oh god, oh god, oh god.*

"It could be a special skill, a favorite book you've read more than once, or an interesting fact about you or your family. For example, my name is Lennox. I'm from Henderson, Nevada. My father is a descendant of a royal family from Namibia, and he had to sneak across the border into Botswana to see the woman who would eventually become his wife and my mother.

"The second time, please share a bit about a leader who inspires you and why."

I flicked my eyes around the room, looking for an escape. I wished I knew how to make myself vomit on demand. My thoughts scampered, trying to find a leader to land on. All I had was Abraham. *No way. Nope. Shit.*

The boy sitting beside me piped up and volunteered to start.

"My name is Kai, and I'm from Missoula, Montana. Something interesting … umm … oh, I know!" He pushed his long bangs back with one hand, exposing a peppering of acne scars on his forehead. "I was accepted to the Hargrove School of Music for piano when I was ten, but I didn't go."

"Why not?" Lennox asked.

"I didn't want to. I wanted to go to a regular school with all my friends. Also, I didn't want to play piano for three hours every day." I glanced over at his hands. They were wide, with long, slender fingers.

"Thanks for sharing that, Kai. Any volunteers to go next? Or should we just go around the circle?"

I held my breath, silently praying for a volunteer. I wasn't ready to go next, and I certainly didn't want to be last. I looked down at the floor, avoiding eye contact. Time stopped moving and sound was sucked away.

"I'll go," a girl in the circle volunteered.

My shoulders relaxed. I was able to breathe again. I was scraping the deep parts of my brain for something to share with the group. I was hoping I could sit here and be forgotten, since we weren't going in any kind of order. After each person spoke, I realized it was getting closer to the point when I would have to speak up. When Lennox asked who hadn't yet introduced themselves, I imagined everyone staring at me. Still, I didn't pull my eyes away from the floor.

"Just go," Kai whispered beside me, nudging my knee with his own. "Trust the process."

I raised my hand and my eyes, looking at Lennox. He nodded, encouraging me to take my turn.

"My name is Zoe, and I'm from …" *A commune in Idaho.* "Billings, Montana. An interesting thing about me … umm … is …" *That I wish Abraham had killed me too.* "Umm … that I am really good at taking care of chickens."

"Do you live on a farm?" Lennox asked.

"Not anymore." *Please don't ask anything else.*

"OK. Thanks for sharing, Zoe."

"I have a question for Zoe," Kai said.

A lump lodged itself in my throat. My oatmeal from breakfast churned in my stomach.

"How many eggs do chickens lay? Like, is it daily, weekly, what? I've always wondered about that."

The lump vanished as I thought about the chickens at the commune who had become like pets. "A hen can lay seven or eight eggs per day," I answered.

"That's a lot of weekly eggs for one family," said a girl in the circle.

"We shared them with a lot of other families," I explained. "Everyone loves farm-fresh eggs." Avoiding the absolute truth without telling an outright lie was getting easier.

"How come you don't live on a farm anymore?" she asked.

At that moment, looking around the circle, I knew exactly

who knew what. I suspected everyone who looked at the ground, or side-eyed this girl, knew who I was. Beside me, Kai gave his head a little shake, subtly trying to tell her not to go there.

"Someone else bought the farm," I said, pushing my lips into a weak smile. It was only as the words came out of my mouth that I realized the double meaning.

"That was a brilliant answer," Kai murmured.

"Why don't you kick off the next round, Zoe?" Lennox suggested.

My mouth went dry, and my hands started to sweat. I wiped them on my jeans and tried to swallow.

"Um, OK. What was the question again?" I croaked, stalling for time.

"Tell us about a leader who inspires you and why."

The sounds in the room roared in my ears: people shifting positions on the floor; the creak of leather as someone took a seat in one of the oversized armchairs; the hum of the light bulbs.

"The leader who inspires me … uh … is my new friend, Shandra."

"That's cool. Why?" Lennox asked.

"Because she has energy for everything in life," I blurted. "She always has a smile on her face. She has my back, even though we haven't been friends for long. She's got her own stuff to deal with, and she does it bravely, without trying to hide her pain."

I folded my hands in my lap, palms up, to allow the sweat to dry.

Lennox nodded. "Thanks for sharing that. It sounds like you've found a wonderful friend, Zoe. Who's next?"

As we progressed around the circle, my heart slowed to a steady thump, thump, thumping. I heard only snippets of what the others said. My memories shifted back to the commune and

Abraham and my father. I fought them away. I wanted to give my head a shake and loosen the hold he had on me. Instead, I sat quietly, head tilted to the floor, and visualized Abraham's face fading into a cloud of dust and drifting away. That would do for now.

After everyone had taken their turn, Lennox led us outside to a garden behind the building. At the far end of the property grew a thick line of trees so large, I could tell from where I stood what they were: pine, birch, and maple. To get into the garden, we passed through an opening in a low stone wall edged in tall wispy grasses. I reached out to let the feathery ends caress my hand. I couldn't resist.

Even the prickliest of weeds can yield the most beautiful flower, my dad had told me as we cleared the invasive orange hawkweed from the commune's gardens.

As a ten-year-old with little capacity to see beyond the literal, I had no idea what he meant. Now I did. I saw those words manifested in Shandra.

We passed rosebushes, boxwoods, and hostas, all in the early stages of turning green after the winter. There were beds of yellow and purple crocuses, the first flower of spring. Amid all the deadness of the last season, their cone-shaped cups called out the arrival of new life. Spring had always been my favorite season.

"This garden is huge!" exclaimed one of the girls.

"It's about a quarter acre, enough space to park forty school buses," Lennox said, turning around to face us while continuing to walk backward. "In the middle of the summer, this place is alive. Birds and bees and butterflies. Squirrels and chipmunks and rabbits. A well-tended garden is an ecosystem unto itself."

"Do we have a destination?" Kai asked.

"We do." Lennox laughed. "Almost there."

He turned his back, and we continued to follow like preschoolers in line after recess. After ten minutes or so, Lennox stopped.

"Here we are," he said, putting his hands on his hips.

I looked around, not understanding what I was supposed to be seeing. We had come to a flat, open area. The grass here had been cut so close to the ground, it was almost nonexistent. A few patio stones were half buried like they'd been placed there a hundred years ago and nature was reclaiming her space.

"Here we are, where?" another student spoke.

"Take a few more steps forward and look down," Lennox advised.

We did as he said, all of us looking at our feet and turning in circles.

"Hold on," Kai's voice broke through the murmur. "It looks like there is a path cut into the grass."

I took a few more steps forward and to my right. When I looked down at my feet, I saw the curve of a path. It was still made of grass, lighter in color than what surrounded it. I lifted my head and could see the walkway laid out before me in twists and turns. It was easy to miss if you didn't know it was there, but once you did, you couldn't unsee it.

"What is this?" I asked.

"It's a labyrinth," Lennox answered.

"Like a maze?"

Lennox shook his head. "Not exactly. A maze has a clear start and finish. A labyrinth doesn't have a solution. It's a journey. You can wander—and wonder—in a labyrinth. When you're only focused on putting one foot in front of the other, following the arcs and turns in the path, it's amazing what your brain will do."

There was some snickering from the group, but I was genuinely intrigued.

"Can we just … go?" I asked.

Lennox nodded, then waved both arms out and wide, inviting us in like a ringleader in a circus.

"Take as long as you need. I know some of you won't want to do this, and that's OK. Give it a try, anyway. We will meet again at lunch. Enjoy the rest of your morning."

thirty-five

LENNOX WALKED INTO THE LABYRINTH. We all stood there, watching him. He dropped his head, put his hands in his pockets, and wandered aimlessly.

I took a few steps forward but followed a different route. I kept my head down, watching the path unfold before me. The birds were singing. I heard girls giggling uneasily and boys jokingly punching each other's not-yet fully formed biceps. I kept walking, and soon, all that background noise faded away.

As I moved, I wondered what I was supposed to be getting out of this exercise. I had no sense of direction, and every now and then I would stop, look up, and try to get my bearings. On the horizon, I could see the line of trees. I saw Kai in the labyrinth with another boy trailing behind. He was off to my left, and when I looked up again after wandering some more, he was in front of me. There was no sense to this path. I had no idea what I was even doing here.

As I continued, images of my parents and my brother flooded my brain. I stopped, bending my body in half, holding my stomach, trying to contain the sensation of deep loss planted there. I took a few breaths in and then let a few breaths out. Slowly, the pressure eased. I stood and resumed walking.

As my arms swung at my side, I paid attention to the flow of blood from my feet to the crown of my head. Through my legs, my groin, my belly, and into my fingers, the burn of grief dissipated. When the flow reached my heart, I filled it with love and visualized that love flooding the four chambers, implanting itself in the soft, pulsing tissues.

As I continued moving, I heard the crackling of fire. I lifted my nose to the air, like a dog following a scent, but I couldn't smell anything other than grass and the mildew of wet leaves. I turned, trying to find and follow the source of the sound, but in the curvy, unstructured world of the labyrinth, the hiss and crackle of fire came from everywhere. I looked up to find the horizon of trees again, but all I saw was the shape of a man, walking toward me.

I wondered if it was Lennox. The shape shimmered, and he was far enough away that I couldn't make out his features. I kept walking toward him, feeling the pull of an invisible string. I was meant to meet this man. I had something important to say to him, but the words were not yet formed in my mouth.

I sped up, walking with intent and purpose now. As we closed the distance, he turned to his left, as if he meant to avoid me. I mirrored his path, turning right. When he turned toward me again, I ran. He was not getting away this time. He stopped walking, waiting for me to approach. The sizzling of the fire grew louder in my ears. When I was no more than fifty yards from him, the blur of his face cleared. Standing there, waiting with arms open like he was expecting a hug, was my father.

That's impossible. He killed himself when he and Abraham were done with everyone else.

My own voice came to me inside my head, as did Dad's. His voice was gravelly, and I wanted to tell him to clear his throat.

I'll always be with you, Ruth.

You're not here. You're dead.

Are you sure about that? You know the media twists everything.

Not like you did. You convinced yourself to do something

horrible. You let yourself be manipulated into thinking murder was salvation.

Are you sure it isn't? I loved you enough to want to free you from the pain of all that we lost.

The crackling of the fire built until it was raging. I felt the heat radiating from my palms, giving me power.

You're a liar.

I never lied. I was only doing what was best for all of us. I was trying to show you the way to save you from your heartache.

You're a monster. You took everything away from me. You told me that you loved me.

I do love you. I always will. You will always belong to me, Ruth.

I glared at him. He shimmered in front of me, smiling. I held my ground, even though every fiber of my being wanted to rush at him and pound my hands into his chest. Because he was my father, the betrayal ran deep. The grief in my belly knotted itself into a pit. I closed my eyes for a second, turning that pain into strength. I visualized my spirit, my being, racing through my body. This was finally my chance to loosen his—and Abraham's —grip on me.

I'm not Ruth anymore. I'm Zoe. Why didn't you let me be who I truly am? I hate you for what you did. I'm done with you. Forever.

I waved my hand dismissively at him. He stared blankly back. In a corner of my mind, I heard another familiar voice.

Forgive him, Zoe.

I turned toward my mother's voice, but she wasn't there.

Forgive him so you can move forward.

I spun in a circle, searching, but saw nothing but fog.

I don't know how to, Mom.

Yes, you do.

I ... I can't. I'm not ready to forgive him.

I watched my dad's ethereal form fracture in front of me. Eric's death had broken him into little bits, and the only way he could cope was to take us all somewhere else. But instead of helping my dad heal his grief, Abraham used it to convince him death was the only way out. Maybe my dad thought he didn't have a choice, and maybe Mom knew that. She could see he was never going to find a way through his pain.

I pulled my mind away from my anger and watched my dad. The sadness emanated from him in a gray fog, and I felt bad for him. Some pain is too great for even a Kane to handle.

Maybe one day I can forgive you. But not yet.

My dad looked at me and nodded. He blew me a kiss, but I didn't reach out to catch it. In a puff of white smoke, he was carried off on an invisible breeze.

I held on to who my parents and Eric were before our world caved in. I released the last little bits of Ruth still lingering inside my head.

As I walked back out of the labyrinth, I felt calm and strong and ready to live.

Kanes always rise, I whispered.

thirty-six

AT LUNCH, the conversation was animated. Some of the people from my group shared their experiences in the labyrinth. The stories ranged from mundane to spectacularly weird to deeply spiritual. One girl said she felt compelled to dance instead of walk through the labyrinth. Someone else said he found he was able to quiet his mind and he stopped worrying about his grades for a bit. Another person said she quit halfway through because she was dizzy.

I remained silent. In that labyrinth, I left part of my old life behind and was walking into this new life. I wanted to savor every bit of freedom I felt inside and keep it all for myself.

Shandra was at the table with two people from her group, Rowan and Allie, outlining the options for the two hours of free time we were given that afternoon. Among the planned choices: a yoga class, a hike, a visit into town, or another tour of the facility.

"What are you going to do this afternoon, Zoe?" Shandra asked.

I shrugged. "I'm not sure yet."

"I'm going into town with Allie and Rowan. Wanna come?"

"Thanks, but I think I might find a comfy seat and read a book. I want to hang out here for a bit."

The truth was, I was considering going back to the labyrinth. I had felt such a release from the pain of losing everyone and being the only survivor. I wanted more of that.

Shandra used the back of her hands to push her long red curls behind her shoulders. She locked eyes with me, then nodded. "OK. We'll see you later."

I grabbed an iced tea on my way out of the dining room, wandering into the central hall. It looked different in the daylight. Without the fire burning in the fireplace and the buzz of a hundred students, the room felt serene. Sunlight poured in through the wall of windows at the far side of the hall. I walked over and stood in the golden afternoon light, watching the ducks bobbing across the glassy surface of the reservoir.

The shores on this side of the reservoir were lined with tall green grasses. They swayed gently in the breeze, and clouds of insects hovered over the water near the roots of the reeds. A dragonfly zipped in to drink and was gone in a heartbeat. On the far side were nothing but trees.

The air rippled in front of the glass; it was an unusually hot day for late spring. I had heard one of the group leaders say that it was going to be a scorcher for most of the day, but by dinner, a cold front was supposed to move in and cool everything down.

One of the group leaders came in through the glass sliding door at the end of the wall of windows, trailed by eight kids. The cooled air in the room was sucked out, replaced with the sticky, suffocating humidity from outside.

"Storm's coming," the group leader said as she walked past me.

I gazed out, taking in the panoramic view. The sky was blue, with a scattering of white fluffy clouds moving through the sky. There wasn't a hint of bad weather, but within minutes, the wind kicked up, shearing the smooth surface of the water and bending the grasses and reeds in half. Out of the corner of my eye, I caught movement coming from the far side of the reservoir.

Thick clouds moved in. The sky darkened quickly, casting the entire reservoir into shadow. The ducks fled the pond.

I stood rooted to the spot, watching the weather change before my eyes. From the sky to the ground, there was nothing but blackness. A wall of rain slid our way, like a door closing out the world. A roar built outside. The ground rumbled and the windows rattled. My ears popped and my body shuddered.

It took less than a minute for the storm to pass. I had never seen weather move so fast. In the glass's reflection, I saw the lights in the central hall flicker. The gloom passed, allowing the sun to shine through again.

I opened the sliding glass door and made my way to the edge of the reservoir. The grass was heavy from the brief downpour, their tips bent to kiss the top of the water. The air smelled of wet woods and damp earth. I closed my eyes, taking a deep whiff through my nose. A memory came with my exhale. My mom and I, standing at the edge of the river after a late-summer storm. We watched tree branches and leaves race by, the flow of the fat river carrying the bits and pieces of nature to a new place.

Mom, is this how the color green smells?

It's the smell of life, she answered.

I inhaled a few more deep breaths, taking a moment to stay in the memory. A splash in the water made me open my eyes. The ducks were back. The sky was clear. It was time for me to move on. I would not let my mom's sacrifice be wasted. Now I had the chance to rebuild my life.

thirty-seven

I FOUND Shandra in the central hall. She was pouting.

"There's no power anywhere in the center," she said. "One of the leaders heard lightning from the storm hit a transformer."

We heard power had not only been knocked out where we were, but in the nearby town, too. We would be fine, the leaders assured us, but we would probably not have power until the final day of the retreat.

Everyone was gathered in the central hall. Jackson and Mandy handed out flashlights, but they ran out long before they got to Shandra and me.

"If you need to go to your rooms, please pair up with another set of roommates who have a flashlight," Jackson announced. He stood in front of the fireplace, clipboard in hand again. "I know you'll be tempted to use your phone flashlights, but remember, we have no power to charge them. Get what you need and then return here for another head count."

"I have a flashlight in my backpack," Shandra told me. "Will you come with me to get it?"

I nodded.

"Are you always this prepared?"

"No. My dad is always this overprotective." She rolled her eyes. "I had to stop him from trying to pack flares. He snuck a full-on first aid kit into my suitcase."

Shandra looked over at me, her eyes searching mine. "Are you OK with ... with me talking about him?"

It took me a second to clue in. I checked in with myself, surprised that I didn't feel the sting of loss and jealousy right away.

"I won't be able to hide from these conversations forever." I shrugged. "I'm happy you still have a dad to talk about."

Shandra linked her arm with mine, and together, guided by the thin light on her phone, we made our way to our room. As we passed through the double doors leading to the dormitory, we heard the murmur of voices coming from the dorms. At the turn in the stairs, lights sprayed the walls, bouncing off the ceiling like searchlights. The hall was filled with students also using their phone lights, despite being warned not to, and chatting away like this was a summer camp adventure.

The flashlight Shandra's dad had packed was like a brick with a light on the end. It was bright enough to wash the entire hallway in a white glow. A stream of other students joined us, following us to the central hall like mice following the Pied Piper.

"Well, this is a bummer," Shandra said, plopping down in one of the oversized leather armchairs. "I guess there won't be any exploring the town for us today."

I sat on the thick arm of the chair, and Shandra shifted over.

"Squeeze in," she said, patting the narrow space beside her.

I hesitated. I was caught off guard, repeatedly, by this girl who was trying to be my friend.

"C'mon, you'll totally fit," Shandra said, misunderstanding my uncertainty.

I slid from the arm into the chair. I sank into the aged and well-worn leather, my legs pressed together, trying not to crowd Shandra.

Jackson was still in front of the fireplace, hugging his clipboard.

"The plan has changed for the day," he announced. "All

activities will now be taking place either here in the central hall or outdoors, at least until it gets dark.”

“We also need volunteers in the kitchen,” Mandy called out from the other side of the room. “We have a ton of refrigerated food that needs to be cooked before it goes bad. So, if anyone has any kitchen experience, knows how to handle a knife, and can cook enormous volumes of food, please come see me.”

“That would be me.” I grinned.

“For real?” Shandra asked.

“Nothing gives you better kitchen experience than cooking for an entire commune. I can work magic with almost-wilted spinach.”

“Ugh, please don’t,” Shandra said, sticking her finger in her open mouth and making gagging sounds.

I started laughing, a deep-rooted laugh that I felt in my entire body. I threw my arms around Shandra, side-squeezing her into a hug, despite the fact I only met her yesterday.

Shandra’s arms wrapped around me. Our cheeks touched and her lips were next to my ear.

“I’m glad I met you,” she whispered. “You were meant to live, Zoe. Just like I am. You may not know why now, but one day, it will be crystal clear. I’m glad you got away. I think you’re amazing, and I’d be lucky to call you my friend.”

In her eyes, I saw all the different versions of me. There was Ruth, not just quietly following the rules, but building an arsenal of skills that would carry her through life. I saw Zoe, who had suffered the worst losses imaginable but found the strength to keep moving forward. Ruth was resourceful; Zoe had the guts to act. I wasn’t one or the other. I was both, a swirling harmony of personalities and skills and experience that made me unique. Being different wasn’t bad; it was actually kind of awesome.

“I’m honored to be your friend too, Shandra.”

thirty-eight

THE KITCHEN at the conference center, lit by emergency lights running off a generator, was nothing like the small community kitchen we had at the commune. The kitchen I learned to cook in had two old stove/oven combos, a pair of white fridges with stains that were neither identifiable nor ever coming off, a folding table with burn marks and knife scars we used for prep, and an assortment of small appliances that may or may not have been working.

This kitchen was clearly made for large-scale prep. All the appliances were huge and gleaming stainless steel. A side-by-side walk-in fridge and freezer took up half of one wall; a gas stove with eight burners, a griddle, and a hood filled another. Next to the stove stood two built-in double ovens. The third wall held shelves where all the plates, mugs, glasses, and serving dishes were stacked; this was also home to the dishwasher. A stainless steel prep table owned the center of the room. Above the table, every cooking utensil imaginable hung from hooks; under the surface of the table were nested pots, deep rectangular pans, sauté pans of all sizes, and cookie sheets.

Mandy and another leader, Ameer, were pulling food out of the fridge.

"Can these last a day or two without a fridge?" Mandy asked, holding up two heads of cabbage.

"Vegetables and fruit should be OK." Ameer nodded. "We need to cook all the meat, though."

For twenty minutes, it was chaos as we piled clear bags filled with chicken legs, cut pieces of beef, and deli meats onto the prep table. Arms and bodies were everywhere. I jumped in, sorting the food so we could see exactly what we had. Laid out in front of us was all the food meant to sustain us for the next two days.

The kitchen came alive. Ameer, whose family owned a restaurant, made his way over to the stove, ovens, and deep fryers, lighting the gas with a whoosh. More than twenty volunteers showed up, and we were divided into crews. Aprons were handed out. Ameer gave us all a safety briefing. Pats of butter sizzled on the flat griddle. Eggs cracked into bowls were whisked into a scramble. I fell into a rhythm as I chopped and sliced carrots, cucumbers, and mushrooms. The familiar camaraderie of the kitchen crept over me, and I remembered how good it felt to be part of doing something useful.

"Yo, Zoe!" I heard someone call from the other end of the prep table.

I looked up and saw Kai smiling at me, waving a knife. I smiled back, hoping the red in my cheeks would be mistaken for exertion.

Kai worked his way over to where I was standing. He pulled an onion out of a bag and was about to start cutting.

Without thinking, I put my hand over his to stop him.

"If you put those in the freezer for fifteen minutes, you won't cry."

"Oh, I'm good." He smiled, slicing into a fat, shiny, white onion.

Within seconds, my eyes were burning and tearing. Kai's eyes were dry and clear.

"How ...?"

"They don't bother me." He shrugged. "I have the same

tolerance for spicy food. I can go inferno hot without a single twitch."

"That's not weird at all," I snarked.

Kai focused on slicing another onion. He was quiet, and I thought maybe I had offended him. I was about to apologize when he grinned.

"Not any weirder than wearing the same ugly-ass dress as everyone else you know."

I gripped the knife in my hand, waiting for the rush of humiliation. When I turned to say something, he was head down, slicing away, but his body shook with laughter. For a second, I was pissed off that he found humor in what had happened to me and my family. But something in the air between us calmed me. He wasn't being mean; he was trying to make me feel normal. It was working.

"OK, piano man, it's on."

Kai continued smiling as we prepped the vegetables. The ten of us at the table fell into easy chatter, each sharing things about our lives, complaining about parents and school, and talking about plans for the future. I surprised myself, being able to talk about my mom and dad without the vise around my heart that had been there for months.

When we were done with the vegetables, I walked over to the freezer, pulling the handle to open the door. With a shiver, I stepped inside. It was mostly empty. I counted two 10 lb. bags of mixed vegetables, five sleeves of hamburgers with twenty-four patties each, a single bag of 150 hot dogs, and to my delight, six vats of ice cream. When I picked up one of the bags of veggies, the contents already felt soft.

"Um, this stuff is melting already," I announced.

Mandy poked her head in the door, looking around. She pulled the lid off one of the vats of ice cream. I could see the melt dripping from the lid.

"Hmmm," she mumbled. "I guess we have to tackle this now, before it's too late. Zoe, can you get a rolling cart?"

As soon as I wheeled over one of the carts stored in the corner of the kitchen, Mandy loaded it up with all the ice cream. She instructed other students to fill the other carts with bowls and spoons.

"OK!" Ameer called out. "Let's get this stuff to the central hall. Looks like we're having ice cream for dinner!"

I started pushing my cart, and Kai appeared by my side to help.

"I can push this on my own," I protested.

"Oh, I know. I just want to be near the caramel ribbon when it's opened. This is about me helping me." He smirked.

It was the right move. Once we were in the central hall and Mandy announced the plan, we were swarmed.

"Oh my god, this is *so* good!" Shandra moaned, licking the last bit of cookie dough ice cream off her spoon. "Ice cream for supper is the dream. You are my hero."

I couldn't wipe the smile off my face.

thirty-nine

BY THE TIME all the food was cooked and put into the freezer that was now serving as a very cold fridge, with a wish and a prayer that it wouldn't spoil, I was ready for sleep.

When I emerged from the kitchen after making sandwiches, then skewering beef and vegetables for what felt like hours, I was surprised to discover the sun had not yet set. Without noticing, we had passed from the dark nights of winter to the late dusk of spring.

I wandered into the central hall and found Shandra, Allie, and Rowan sprawled on a fluffy white rug in front of the fireplace, absent-mindedly flipping through magazines.

"I'm exhausted." I sighed, plopping down next to Shandra.

"At least you got to work off all those ice cream calories," Allie moaned. "I feel like I have a food baby."

"Maybe we should go for a walk," Rowan suggested.

"Nah-uh." I grimaced. "My legs hurt, my arms are sore, and I've got nothing left."

"We're supposed to stay here until our group leaders come," Shandra said.

As soon as the words came out of her mouth, Lennox appeared.

"Hey, everyone, you need to find your group leader. We are moving outside for an activity. Zoe, can you help me collect the rest of the group?"

With great effort, I pushed myself off the floor. "See you out there," I told my new friends.

Once all the students were assembled in their groups, Jackson led us to a field on the far side of the center. We moved like a herd, and I couldn't see where we were going. I shook my head and tried not to laugh as I listened to Kai and another student from my group, Mark, trying to outdo each other by comparing the most meat they had eaten at one sitting.

When we stopped and spread out, I saw we had come to a circle of benches built around a firepit. An anvil settled on my chest, choking the breath out of me. My heart pounded. I was lightheaded and my legs shook. I tried to ask for help, but only a squeak passed my lips.

Kai must have heard me, because he turned around.

"Zoe, are you OK?" he asked, touching my arm.

I recoiled from the sensation. "Don't touch me," I hissed. He pulled his hand back. I saw him looking around before my vision blurred.

I knew what was happening, but I was powerless to stop it. Dr. Duxelles had told me I should get to a safe place if I was having a panic attack, but here, amid a hundred students gathered in an open field, there wasn't anywhere for me to go. I started turning my wrists, like I was stretching them, trying to release the tension.

"Zoe, listen to my voice …" Kai's voice came to me like I was standing inside a bubble. He stepped over the bench to stand by my side.

"Think of five things you can see. Don't say anything, just look."

I willed my eyes to move. I looked down and saw my runners, the ones Lottie bought me for this retreat. I saw someone's twirled laces. Then grass, a three-leaf clover, and a bent zipper pull on a boy's hoodie.

When I was done, I nodded.

"Now, think of four things you could touch."

My hair, my jeans, the wood of the bench, the spot of sticky ice cream I missed on the outside of my right hand.

I nodded again.

"Now, three things you can hear."

His voice. A bug buzzing nearby. Logs being split.

"When you've got that, move on to two things you can smell."

Hint of skunk. Freshly chopped onions.

"One thing you can taste."

"That caramel ribbon I licked off my thumb," I said. My voice didn't shake, and my breath came back. The weight from my chest was gone. "How … how did you do that? How did you know?"

"I get panic attacks too," he admitted. "This is the only thing that helps me out of it."

"You're brilliant."

"Yeah, I am," he boasted, "but I can't take credit for that. I had a really good therapist."

For a second, I thought Kai was joking, but when I looked at him, he was shuffling his feet in the grass. Kai ran a hand through his thick brown hair, rubbed the back of his head, then brought his hand back through to the front. His hair was now sticking up all over the place.

"What's the trigger?" he asked.

"The firepit. All my stuff was burned in the commune's firepit before they gave me my new name. I'm not sure how I'll be once the fire starts. Can you … would you … sit with me?" I swallowed to keep my voice from cracking.

"Yeah, sure," he answered. "Let's move to the back. We'll have an easy escape route if we need one."

Kai lowered himself to the bench, placing encouraging and

gentle pressure on my shoulder. I sank down onto the worn wood. For now, I felt shielded, sitting in the back row with Kai and the rest of my group.

I took a deep breath and surveyed the pit and the benches. Students were sitting down and checking their phones. I looked at as many faces as I could without being noticed. How many of us are broken and hiding it? I would never know. It's impossible to know what is going on in someone else's head.

And at that moment, I realized nothing I could have done would have stopped my father from making his choice and doing what he did. I was going to be angry with him for a long time. Forgiveness might never come, and I was okay with that.

forty

TWO WEEKS LATER, lying in bed and still processing everything that had happened at the retreat, my eyes were getting heavy when I felt a poke in my side.

"Zoe … are you asleep?"

I rolled onto my side. Chelsea was lying on the air mattress on the floor of my bedroom, head propped up with a bent arm.

I opened one eye to look at her. Her eyes sparkled, not a hint of fatigue. I knew this look well by now. It usually meant she had a brilliant idea that was going to get her into trouble. Or me. Or all of us.

"I was almost there." I sighed, rubbing my eyes.

"Me too," Shandra said from her mattress on the other side of me.

I smiled to myself in the semidark. Never in my life did I think I'd be sandwiched between my two best friends. Lottie was the one who suggested I invite them for a sleepover. After dinner, the four of us spread out around the living room to watch a movie. Shandra and I were on the couch with a giant bowl of popcorn between us. Chelsea took one of the oversized armchairs, sitting sideways with her legs draped over one arm, munching on a bag of licorice. Lottie settled into the other armchair with a bag of caramel M&M's on her lap. I was feeling so good about life, I sent Gary an email to let him know he could catalogue me as one of his success stories.

You've figured out who you are, he wrote back. *Now move forward with that. And **you** deserve all the credit.*

"I just thought of something," Chelsea said.

"Can't it wait until morning?"

"It is morning." She laughed.

I picked up my phone, an end-of-the-school-year gift from Lottie, and looked at the time: 2:34 a.m. We had been talking until about thirty minutes ago.

"This is important," Chelsea urged.

"Oh god, are we going to talk about boys again?" Shandra groaned, bringing her fists to her eyes. "Can we not?"

"You were the one who wanted to gossip about Tristan and Kai," I pointed out.

Chelsea and Tristan had gone out on one date, where they mutually decided to just be friends. Kai and I kept in touch after he went home to Missoula. My long-distance crush was cut short when Kai told me he and Mark had started dating.

I pushed my quilt down over my knees and sat up, crossing my legs. Shandra and Chelsea did the same. I still couldn't get used to Shandra's short hair, with her loose curls falling just below her ears. We went to her favorite salon the weekend after we came home from the retreat. She had cut off all her hair while I had the ends of my long hair dip-dyed bright purple. When Shandra was done squealing over the color, she pointed out that women who ate ice cream for dinner could do whatever they wanted. But I knew she really wanted a fresh start. We were both becoming experts in the do-over.

I waited.

"OK. Go," I said impatiently.

"I think we should play a round of Fortunately, Unfortunately," Chelsea said.

"Huh? Now?" We had played that game sitting around the bonfire at the retreat. I had never played it before, but the twisted, nonsensical tale that spun out as each person took their turn had me laughing to tears.

"Yeah. I have an inspiration."

"Chels, I love you, but can we just go to sleep?"

"Humor me," she pleaded.

Shandra got up, then my bedroom flooded with light from my bedside lamp.

"OK," Chelsea started. "Fortunately, I finally got around to cleaning out my room."

"Unfortunately," Shandra continued, "you found an abandoned pudding cup buried in your closet."

I yawned but gave in.

"Fortunately," I added, "the pudding is full of preservatives and had zero mold."

"Unfortunately—" Shandra started.

"Hey! It's supposed to go back to Chelsea."

"Just play," Chelsea said. She nodded to Shandra, and I thought I saw a look pass between them.

"Unfortunately, a shoebox fell on your head while you were in your closet."

"Fortunately," Chelsea continued, "the lid fell off and the contents spilled out."

I opened my mouth to take my turn, but Shandra cut me off.

"Unfortunately, you had to meet your math tutor and couldn't go through the box."

"Fortunately, when I got home, I took the time to examine the contents."

"Unfortunately, you found a poem you wrote to a boy you liked in third grade and realized you'll never be a writer."

"Fortunately—"

"Wait! Who was the boy?" I blurted out.

Chelsea ignored my question. She reached into her overnight bag. I watched her root around, digging for something.

"Fortunately," she went on, "I found this." She pulled her hand out of the bag in a flourish. She handed me a frame, which held the photo of the two of us, dressed in Victorian costumes.

"I made you a copy." She beamed.

In the photo, I saw two seven-year-olds smiling wildly, playing dress-up, but also hurrying to grow up, blissfully oblivious to the future. When I tore my eyes away from the picture, both Chelsea and Shandra were wiping away their tears.

"When the fair opens this summer, we'll go and get a new photo. Of the three of us," Chelsea announced.

I lay back down on my mattress, hugging the framed photo to my chest. I pulled the corner of my quilt up to my face to catch my own tears. The hole in my heart left from the loss of my parents and Eric and everyone in the village was never going to fully close, and I was going to be OK with that.

People make poor choices when steeped in sadness. I learned to forgive my father for his actions, but I also learned to work through my guilt for surviving and truly believed I deserved to live. Even though I was called Ruth for more than half my life, I had always been Zoe, just on hold for a while. I was a Kane, and a Kane always rises.

follow the author

Instagram|Threads|Facebook
@authordanagoldstein
Website
danagoldstein.ca

Join my newsletter to stay in touch and learn about upcoming titles and events.
danagoldstein.substack.com

For more information scan the QR code.

acknowledgments

As I close the manuscript for my seventh (7th!!) book, I realize some of the people I want to thank have been part of my writing world from the very start. I am so fortunate to have the best of the best in my circle.

Thank you to my developmental editor, Zoey Duncan, who took on this mess of a book as she navigated a new job and a toddler. Your gentle, but no-nonsense, approach to editing is much appreciated, especially when I know some of what you had to sift through was absolute garbage. Once again, you have had a hand in making this book better.

I must thank Jennifer Sommersby, my copy editor, who went through this manuscript line by line while she was launching a new business endeavor and moving house. I should add that there was some weird language and formatting issues going on with the document. I am truly sorry for the chaos in the pages.

Thanks to proofreader Catherine Szabo, who always gets my books ready for the final step.

Thank you to Julie Boake from Awedity Creative for designing another spectacular and AI-free cover. Your ability to take my mutterings and musings and make the perfect cover continues to astound me. You'd think after seven books, I'd be better at expressing what my vision is, but I need to live with the fact I will always be vague and confused.

Big props to my husband who read ten out of the fifteen

(15!!!) drafts of this book. I couldn't ask for a more supportive partner. I appreciate you beyond measure.

To my sons, Mason and Westin, one of whom read the fourteenth draft of Raising Kane and had some fantastic input. The other one, well, I love him as a mother should and forgive him for not reading this book at all.

And finally, to all the wonderful readers and supporters, I thank you for continuing to buy *every single book* I put out. I think of all of you as I am writing, hoping the next project will be as loved as the last.

xo Dana

about the author

Dana Goldstein is the author of three memoirs: *The Girl in the Gold Bikini, Murder on my Mind*, and *Spent*. She is also the author of a middle grade duology: *Shift* (2023, Young Dragons Press) and *Flow* (2024, Young Dragons Press). In 2024 she published her debut contemporary fiction, *Katya Noskov's Last Shot*. Her short story, *Malcolm and the Magpie* was included in *The Kids Short Story Advent Calendar* (Hingston & Olsen). Her work has appeared in *Write* magazine, and *Women Writers, Women's Books*. Dana lives, creates and writes from her home in Calgary, Alberta, Canada.

goodreads.com/authordanagoldstein

instagram.com/authordanagoldstein

threads.com/authordanagoldstein

also by dana goldstein

<u>Fiction</u>

Katya Noskov's Last Shot

<u>Memoir</u>

The Girl in the Gold Bikini

Murder on my Mind

Spent

<u>Middle Grade Fiction</u>

Shift

Flow